A Family's Revenge

The Third Book by Robert Segulin

Author of

The Promise

The Next Mission

the Fall of an American Hero

This book is dedicated to my daughter who has given me love and inspiration in how she has lived her life so far. I only hope that this book deserves her admiration like I have for her.

This is a book of the perseverance of one man, the nephew of an American hero. This one person took the whole of what was that the reason of his uncle's death, and made it his revenge!

CHAPTER ONE

It has been six years after the one person that meant the most to me back then, that I remembered with a sip from my glass of scotch, and a nod of appreciation. Rick James was an American hero and the one man that has given me the inspiration to move on. Every year around the July Fourth Holiday, I remember what I did for Rick and what he did for me. This was a time in my life and for so many others that would agree to the fact that without the help of Rick James that few of us in our little circle of family and friends would be here today! The fact that I cannot talk to him, and to be part of his amazing life anymore, has made me so sad but also happy that I have had the once in a lifetime chance to be in his life, and him in my life.

Six years ago, on another very pleasant Fourth of July day just like this one has turned out to be, the sun was now high in the sky and a slightly warm breeze was blowing through those same tall pine trees as they did not so long ago. I was just sitting on my patio remembering the life that I had with Rick when I heard a voice!

The voice that I heard was not one that I could not forget, but one that I have not heard in a long time.

What I heard was, "hey Uncle Bob! How are you doing today?" That phrase and that voice made me remember so much that I never wanted to forget the history of my friend Rick and that of his nephew Charlie.

I turned so slowly as to not make a motion in any distinct way that he might disappear for I thought that at my age, and the ability of my mind has, made me think of what was to be and what was not here.

As I turned towards the sound of his voice, I looked at part of the reason that I followed Rick to St. Louis. Yes, it was Charlie. I could not believe the fact that he was here in Ohio on my patio.

I was speechless at this moment and could only remember the last day on this patio six years ago, I was looking up at his Uncle Rick. Sadness of that memory quickly disappeared when Charlie started to speak again.

Charlie said, "so this is your patio and your flowers, I guess yours and my uncle stories were real." I laughed and said do you think that we would make sitting here and having a drink and looking at my flowers up. When he shook his head, in that instant I remembered Rick would shake his head in the same way.

So many memories started to fill my head at that moment of the different encounters and the many people that we met on our journeys together.

As I was just about to get up to either shake his hand or give him a hug that I needed I think more than Charlie right now.

Charlie sat down right next to me and reached over to put his arm around me and let me know that he misses him also. Tears of both joy and sadness filled my eyes when he did and said that. I grabbed his other hand and shook it and told him that Rick would be so proud of how you have turned out now. Charlie said, "that he knows in his heart that his uncle is always with him on every mission that he is on."

I quickly turned to him and said, Mission! Charlie said, "yes sir I have enlisted a few years ago, and just last year have been assigned to a special operation unit that is about to go to Afghanistan and Iraq, plus many other places around the Middle East and Europe." This time I shook my head and said that what you are doing is not what your uncle would want you. Charlie said, "that he understood that if he was still around that he would not allow me enlisting and becoming a special op like him." And I then asked him that how did your mother allow you to do it. He said, "that when he turned eighteen that he enlisted and just left a note to her and his sister giving his reasons and apologizing to them."

I sat back in my chair and was so amazed at how he looked and what he did even though it was not what his mother and uncle would approve of, I truly was proud of him and his decision. I told Charlie that I did understand why he did it and I was very proud of him and hoped he would be careful and to above all complete your mission.

Charlie smiled! As he smiled I saw his Uncle Rick smiling at me and again thought of how I truly do miss him.

I told Charlie that if there is anything that I can do to help you with the mission that I feel you are about to embark on, I will try to do whatever I can at my age.

I told him, to just remember when Rick and I went all over the country I was a touch younger but now, I can do things that may help you without running and shooting people. Charlie gave a chuckle and said, "to me that he did not want me to be running and shooting, but he may need me to visit his mother and sister to explain what I have to do now." I looked at him and said that I will make plans now to visit them very soon and I will let them know why you must do what you are about to do. Even though I said to Charlie, I have no idea what it is exactly. And he said to me, "that someday you will understand as my family will."

Charlie and I sat for a long time and talked about his family and his uncle. He did not say much of what he has been up to while in the military.

I did not press him about anything and I only wanted to know of his time back home with his family and whatever happened to Stacey. I told him that I always asked your mom but she never said anything about her.

Charlie said, "that right after Uncle Rick passed, she left the area and mom has really not heard anything from her. Mom said that Stacey talking to her just reminded her of Rick and that was something that she could not handle."

I told Charlie that I can feel Stacey's hurt just as I have felt it for so long. I knew that I should have visited St. Louis more than I have, but every time I do I feel the loss I have and that I will never find a friend and a comrade like your Uncle Rick. Again, Charlie lowered his head and shook it in agreement.

After that conversation, I asked Charlie to tell me of his mother and his sister and what is happening in their lives now. Charlie then said, "can I have a scotch over ice, and I will start." I could only laugh and tell him that your uncle and I never had a drink together and I will be so happy and proud to have you have one with me today. I poured and he toasted to Rick James a true American hero. I lifted my glass and added a man who loved his family. Then Charlie formed a tear and smiled.

CHAPTER TWO

Then Charlie started to inform me of what his life was about, and his family's life after I left and that what happen next when he entered the military.

After many drinks and about two hours of conversation Charlie and I started a new bond that was to take us on another journey, but this time with me here and him somewhere else.

He was telling me about the day he left for the military when he began to write the note telling his mother and sister of his decision. At that moment when he first put the pen to the paper, he remembered what his mother told him of when his uncle did the exact same thing and in the same way. Charlie said that even though it was about the same that it was for totally different reasons.

He said that his uncle left because he needed a change, from the constant changes in his life and that he wanted to be part of something stable even if it was a dangerous stable.

I asked Charlie then if you had a completely different reason, you still left in the same way with no warning and discussion of entering the military instead of what might have been on your mother's mind for you instead.

Charlie said, "that he knew what she had hopes for me going to college and becoming a teacher or lawyer, or anything except a soldier."

"But I had a different idea of my life that I wanted to become and what I wanted to accomplish with it.' I looked at him and had a good idea of what his accomplishments will be, but I said nothing about that and only asked him where next.

Charlie said, "that his next mission will take him to different locations with all about the same plan in each area. He also said that if I would please go to his mothers and give her this letter from me." I agreed and asked again where and when will he be home. He just shook his head in a no shake and said, 'that I hope to be done and home soon." I looked at him and said that is not an answer. Charlie then said, "that what he said is about all he could for now."

I told Charlie that you have my number and make sure that someone close has it also and if you ever need me call or text. I will cross an ocean to help you. Charlie smiled and said, "now I understand how you and Uncle Rick did all that you did together." Then he told me that he will be all right and to tell his mom not to worry.

I let him know that I would tell her and your sister plus I will give both a hug from you. Charlie nodded and said, "can we now change the subject."

Again, I told Charlie to be careful and to get in touch when you can. After that, he walked down my walk and went to his ride that was waiting for him.

I had a bad feeling just like Rick used to say, about what he is about to get himself into very soon. I called Josie and let her know that I will be out next week and if will be around from school or not.

I did not mention Charlie on the phone for that is a subject that needs to be discussed in person. She said, "that we will be around and that we cannot wait to see you." I told her to not worry about me being at her house since I already have a hotel for a few days. She said, "that it was not ok but understandable." And we both hung up.

I then wondered what Charlie was up to with this new mission that will take him all over the globe.

CHAPTER THREE

A week went by and the next thing I know I was landing in St. Louis. As I started down the walkway towards the concourse, the only sound that I heard was. Uncle Bob! That was coming from Terri waiting for me at the end. It has been too long and they showed it.

Terri ran up first and then Josie, they both gave me a super hug and Terri grabbed by carryon bag and we were off to their place. Josie said, "with a little sadness in her voice that Charlie is not here." I told Josie that I know and we will talk about his new mission in life. She looked at me and asked, "how did you know?" And I told her that he was at my place a few days ago, and that he is fine. Now let's get home and I will tell you more. Josie just kept looking at me with an uncertain James look in her eyes. As we were driving to their place Josie was very quiet and, Wow! Terri, she would not stop talking. She was asking me questions and answering them also.

She was a beautiful young woman now and I know Rick would be so protective of her. And she just began college and is to be a teacher like her mother.

We arrived at her condominium and I asked her why she did not take me to my hotel, and Josie said, "that she cancelled the room and that I was staying with them." I smiled and said that you are a James. She just smiled back and nodded yes. We all got out of the car and went into the condominium, but as I was walking up her walk I remembered what went on that day six years ago, and how not only did I lose a friend but a comrade in arms. Sadness filled my heart and I could see that both felt the same, for neither talked until we were inside. And boy did Terri talk.

I asked that if I could have just a few minutes with her mother before we go over the last few years that I have not been around. Terri looked at me and knew what I wanted to talk about. Charlie!

We sat in silence for a few minutes and then Josie just cried out, "why Bob! Why did he enlist and why did he not want to have a normal life? And most of all, why does he want to die like his Uncle did." I grabbed her and tried to let her know that he is his own man and that deep down inside he has something that he must do before he can let go of the idea of his uncle passing.

Josie just looked at me and said, "that she does not want Charlie to end up like Rick, killed by the men who he may be chasing."

I told her that Charlie is now chasing demons from that night that have given him a purpose in his life even though it just may have him killed, but I still feel he is not going to let it completely consume him now.

I saw so much of Rick in his eyes when he came by, and in those eyes, was calm and peace, not total hate, for that is what I thought I would have seen instead. I then told Josie that Charlie is now in the special operations strike force that goes all around the globe hunting and eliminating terrorist and their sympathizers. She just looked at me in shock after I told her that.

Josie is a strong woman but with the news of her little boy she then became a bowl of mush. She had no idea of what he was doing only that he was following his uncle in joining the military. I continued with what Charlie had told me of him not making the grade to become a sniper that made Josie give a small smile. I then said that he is in a relatively sort of safe job. He oversees locating the target for the advance unit. What he does is put all the information that every agency has gathered on the target and try to put a scenario of what that person will be up to and where they might be at any time soon. Then with all the information he gives it to the commander and the team goes to the co- ordinance that Charlie feels the target may be. Again, Josie gave a faint smile feeling that he is in the background and not one of the advance team.

She also knew that he was very smart when someone would lose an object he would locate it with reasoning and of a feeling of who lost it and their travels that day.

I agreed with her that what he is doing is about the same, but with people instead of an object. And these people do shoot at you and with that statement Josie became quiet again.

Josie looked up at me and asked, "Bob how is he really?" I told her that the way he left I did give him a bit of a verbal thrashing, but he looks great. Taller than I remember and with a very strong looking body without the bulging muscles but knowing that he was in very good shape. He had such a similar body type as your brother. Josie looked up quickly and said my brother? I said I mean Rick. Josie knew that I was trying to calm down the feelings that we both have right now that we are together and he is not. I went on with telling her of some of the areas and people that he has been too and has encountered. Some of the countries that he went to are not exactly the safest places but I let her know that he told me that his unit always sticks together and no harm comes there way with them all together. Josie just continued with a stare and not much emotion now.

CHAPTER FOUR

After approximately two hours Terri came into the room and said, "enough you two! We all have to go to eat and we all need to know what the other has been up to." Josie and I both laughed and agreed with that notion. I just gave a stare at Terri and could not help seeing a bit of Rick on her face and her similar mannerisms.

We drove to a restaurant not far away, but we drove past the park that it all happened in and not a word was spoken as we did. I could only feel the emotion of what had gone on that day and how I lost a great friend and a comrade in arms. Josie, I felt thought of her brother and Terri her uncle. And all of us the loss of losing Charlie to his revenge that now filled his soul. No matter what I said to Josie of how safe Charlie was she knew better and Terri lost her best friend and brother to demons that she did not understand or wanted to admit to herself that she had her share also.

We arrived at the restaurant and as we were seated Terri started the conversation with what she has been up to first.

She began with her graduating from high school and starting college and wanting to be a teacher like her mother.

I told her that what she was doing not only is a fantastic career but a showing of admiration of what her mother has done with her life. I let both know how happy I was to have could become friends with all of them, Terri interrupted with, "and family, right Uncle Bob?" I said yes, a family that I inherited through the friendship of Rick. I am so proud of you Terri and I know you will become a great teacher and someday have a family of your own. She smiled and Josie just nodded because she was in a daze listening to the two of us and I only could imagine what was on her mind right now. Probably the same feeling that years ago, that she had when Rick left for the military and she did not hear from him for some time of what he was doing and was he safe.

A moment later Josie seemed to just snap out of her deep thought and quickly spoke up and said, "you all know what I have been doing these past years, the same thing I have been for years raising a family and teaching plus taking care of the home." Terri and I smiled and told her how great of a job that she has done with all of that. Well, I guess it is my turn next to bore both of you.

I started a few days after I left them and returned to where my daughter was at the time and her mother.

The medical staff told me that it would be to my benefit to have some people around in case I relapsed and needed help.

So, I stayed for about a year in New York, during that time my daughter started to make plans to go back to New Jersey because the barn was up and running again.

This time not as a huge training barn, because Samantha said that most of the boarders have not come back now yet. And most of the horses have escaped and they have been trying to find them. After she informed us of her leaving I felt that maybe I should try to go back to where I lived. After all this trouble ended I put my stuff into storage.

I eventually left and went back to Ohio and back to the apartment complex. The whole place has changed some but not in design but with many of the original residence gone. I could not believe it but my apartment was empty and I moved back into it. I bought a couple of new chairs for the patio and went to see if the beverage store was open, and yes it was. So, for years now I tried to have a normal life as it was before. But not a day would go by that I would not look up over my fence when I heard a voice thinking it was someone from before that lived here.

I went back to going to what horse shows that were going on that my daughter was in and visited family and made some new friends in the complex.

And anyone that I would talk to in the complex would always bring up that day when this group of units stood up to the terrorist and won.

And they would try and thank me, but before they could I would always tell of the brave that died at that time in our countries history and those that made a difference in this town.

So, I ended my story with the story that brought us together and now again we are back together, all except Charlie said Josie in an oh so sad voice.

CHAPTER FIVE

Josie excused herself so she could go to the restroom. Right after she left the table Terri moved closer to me and asked me how is Charlie? I told her that when he was by my apartment that day, he looked very good. He was very talkative and did not seem to have a cloud of demons over his head at that time. I told her that he did miss you and that he was sorry for the way he left. Charlie admitted that he left his mother almost the same way that your uncle left her so many years ago. But he did say that his leaving was different as Uncle Rick left his surroundings and Charlie said that he has a mission to fulfill. Terri asked me what mission? I told her that what he does now, is making so many people safer than before.

Terri came even closer now and said how is he making us safer? I told her of his duties in the special operations unit that he is in. Terri pulled back! Special Operations Unit! I thought you said he was safe. I told her that he goes over all the information that is gathered and decides where and when to find and eliminate the enemy.

He rarely goes into battle unless his unit is attacked which he told me was not likely because of the advance unit usually stops any attack before it would reach headquarters.

She then asked, "where is Charlie now?" I told her that I do not know because any place that he goes to is top secret and he could not even give me a country that he was heading to after he left my area. All I know is that he has been to so many countries and helped eliminate so many of the people that attacked us on that day.

Terri asked, "if they caught or killed the one that, uh, was responsible for Uncle Rick." I told her that Charlie said he constantly keeps looking for any information on him, for Charlie said that is his main reason for enlisting. And that Syeed is his main demon that he has in his head. And one he vowed to get!

Terri then told me, "that she thought of going into the military for the reason of going after Syeed, just like Charlie has done. But I knew my mother would not survive with both of us going into the service so I felt that college and becoming a teacher would be better. She also said that in college some courses that she is going to start taking was of law enforcement just in case I feel the need to join the F.B.I or some other agency to help with our fight for a safer country."

I was pulled back this time and told her a teacher is helping us be safer by helping students understand what freedom is to us and how so many other countries wish for our type of freedom.

She smiled and said, "that she could join the C.I.A. and help teach around the world!" I did not smile at that statement from her. I told her to just be a good daughter and sister and when the time comes when your brother comes back home you all will be safe together. Plus, there is no need for the two of you to both be chasing the same demon. One right now is enough! Terri, I have made peace with the fact that one day whether it is Charlie or some other person, will find and end the demons that we all have with that man.

Josie came back to the table and asked what you two were talking about so close as to not let anyone hear your conversation. I said not much just the same old what we are up to, and Terri smiled and agreed. Well, Josie knew what was up and she pretended not to so we would not continue a conversation that she does not want to hear.

We finished dinner and Josie said, "that we should get going for she wants to get to bed early so we all can get up and have a good breakfast before we go to the cemetery. Josie said that at a certain point when the sun rises up in the sky it cast a shadow from a tree nearby with its branches looking as if it is covering the grave site in an umbrella like way of protection from any more, evil."

With that statement, we all began to have a tear drop form in each of our eyes. One that gave so much protection will have the trees shadow now to protect him.

We all got up and left the restaurant together holding each other all in silence for none could now talk with tears in our eyes and our throats congested up.

CHAPTER SIX

Everyone was already up and in the kitchen when I came out of the bathroom and as I entered the area by Josie and Terri a knock was heard at the front door. Josie had such a glow with a great big smile, and Terri started to smile and asked her mother, could it be. I knew what she meant by that question, was it Charlie. Josie ran to the door and when she opened it her face became saddened with who was not at the door. A man around Josie's age and my height stood at the door looking at Josie and Terri with amazement with the reaction that they gave of him by the door. He asked them who did you expect, you knew I was coming with you to the cemetery this year. Josie glanced at me with I am sorry face and turned back to the man at the door and said I am so sorry but I was hoping it might be Charlie.

Then the man understood her look of dissatisfaction with his presence at the door. He came in and said hello to Terri and gave Josie a hug. Josie immediately turned back to me and introduced him as a teacher friend. I knew better than think that she would not get with someone, especially after her ex and Rick being gone. And now Charlie!

While Josie and Terri continued to get the food, ready I talked to this new friend of Josie's. I felt that he was good for her and that she was probably very good for him also.

We all ate and left for the cemetery all in one vehicle. When we arrived the new friend of Josie put his arm around her and I did the same to Terri for the two of them were already with tears rolling down each cheek. When we were just in front of the site I could see the shadow that Josie spoke of and how its branches formed a sort of hand like symbol around his headstone.

With that site, I now had tears forming in my eyes and a clogged-up throat. I held tight to Terri not for her steadiness but for mine. I began to have so many memories rush through my mind that I felt weakened by those Images.

As we all stood by the grave site a cool breeze came through and the trees that gave off the shadow swayed and made the shadow now look as if it was patting the headstone. I remembered the knife that Rick would tap for luck and I thought the branches were patting the stone in the same sort of way.

I looked over to Josie and she was shaking, yet smiling. I was thinking of what she might be feeling now and as I continued to look at her she turned around and smiled even more. Her mother's intuition is telling her that she is feeling Charlie's presence right now. She knows in her heart even though she cannot see him that he is somewhere close by.

And she was right on with her feeling, because approximately a hundred or so yards away looking through binoculars was Charlie watching all of us at the site. He wanted to be closer but knew that it would not be any easier to leave once he was up close to his mother and sister. He was about to leave on another mission that would take him half way around the world to try and find another target. He so wanted to just run to them and hug both until he had to leave, but he knew his mother would not let him go again.

Josie turned to me then and took in a deep breath and put her hand on her heart as she smiled and said Charlie. I nodded at her and gave a brief smile and then a look of uneasiness for I felt that some other person or persons were also close by. But these people were not looking through binoculars; one of them was looking through a scope that was attached to a sniper rifle.

Josie saw my face and started to come towards me and at that exact time a rifle being fired was heard and the bullet that was meant for Josie instead hit the bottle of cold beer that I put on top of the headstone. I moved to Josie and Terri and brought them to the ground as Josie's friend had no idea of what just happened. I got back up and pulled him down also. I turned behind us and only hoped that if Charlie was back there that he was safe. And at the same moment that I hoped that Charlie was safe, Josie yelled to Charlie to run and be safe my son.

And that is exactly the opposite of what he did, and what he did was run to where he thought the shot came from.

He was with a few others and they took off after him in pursuit of the shooter. In his mind, that person or persons will not get away from him now.

We all went behind the headstone and Terri said, "even now Rick is protecting all of us." I smiled at her and agreed. I felt that it should be safe now so I told them to get back to the car and that I will be right behind them. Josie looked at me and said Bob your war is over. I nodded and then pulled out my 9mm and motioned for them to leave. I told her when Charlie is home, then my war will be over.

Josie's friend was now totally confused at what just happed and the only words that Josie said to him was, "move it! I do not want to lose another man that I care for." And with those words, they ran to the car and took off. Terri screamed at her mother and said what about Uncle Bob? Josie then told her that he will be ok, because he is with your brother Charlie and the two will get whoever tried to shoot us.

Josie was right with that Charlie was with me now and two huge friends of his. I asked Charlie if he knew the direction of the shot and he said that it seemed to come from that mausoleum over by that big oak tree. I told him that those two go to the left of it and that you and I go right. Charlie said, "not that I do not doubt your abilities now Uncle Bob, but why not just stay back and cover our six."

28

I told him that I made a promise before the battle to your uncle that if I made it out and he did not that I would do whatever to protect his family.

So, Charlie you are stuck with this old man now. His two friends gave thumbs up and took off to the left. And Charlie smiled and said, "let's not wait for them, so move it Bob." Those words again brought back memories and I knew he was right, so I got moving and kept a sharp look out for what may be ahead.

I heard a commotion over in the direction of his two friends and Charlie and I took off together to check it out. When we arrived, we saw the two military friends with a knife to the throat of one of the men that were shooting at the site. The other one was dead and Charlie thanked them for leaving one alive so he can find out why his family.

The man of Middle Eastern decent lay on the ground and when we came up to him, he smiled and said that your war may be over now, but Syeed's war is just beginning again. Then he bit into a pill and his mouth foamed up and he was dead.

I told Charlie to get out of the area and that I will take your mother and sister away from here until we both feel that it might be safe for the two of them to return. We shook hands and with his friends said when needed I will be there.

I went back to the condominium; it was a long walk but it was what I needed to have before I saw Josie. I knew that she would have so many questions and that I do not have the answers yet.

CHAPTER SEVEN

When I made it back to the condominium, Terri came running out and came up to me asking if I was ok. I told her yes and that I need to talk to your mother right away. Terri then said that Charlie was, there, wasn't he? I said yes and that he had a couple of friends with him. She asked what happened to the people that tried to shoot us. I told her that Charlie's friends took care of them. She then said how Charlie is and is he coming here also. I told her that he has a mission and that we will see him when it is over.

Josie came out of the condominium and the only words she spoke was, "is he safe?" I told her yes and that the people that tried to shoot us are not. Then she asked, "if he coming here?" I told her as I told Terri that he has a mission and that he will return when it is over.

She then said, "how about you Bob; are you doing ok." I told her that my ticker just had a good workout and that I am doing fine now.

Josie came up to me and put her arms around me and in my ear said…"it was Syeed, wasn't it!"

I said not him but that he sent men to finish his war. Josie said, "that I thought after Rick, that it would be over."

I let her know that I had the same idea and that we had seen the last of his kind. But what we both thought was wrong and that we are in another battle, this time without Rick. Josie said, "but this time we are in with Charlie!" I smiled and agreed.

We all went into the condominium and I then began to inform Josie and Terri that they would have to go. Josie's friend asked me why they must go away; the police can protect them can't they. I told him that if they want to do harm to the two of them that the police cannot prevent them from doing what they have in mind for them. He still did not understand, so Josie sat down with him and explained why. She told him the story of what happened years ago, in July and how Rick and I gave our all and the police, Guard, and residence and with all that they still got to me and my family.

Then he understood and said that he will go with her to help. Josie said that she does appreciate his offer but that she cannot put anyone else in harm's way now or in the future. He agreed with her thinking but he still could not help but want only the best for her and Terri. After he left Josie and I planned of where they should go to and how they would get there. I thought that maybe it would be a good idea to fly to New York with my daughter's mother or to New Jersey with Samantha.

Josie said, "that she was thankful of my offer to go to their place, and said that it may be better if Terri and I go where no one will be put in jeopardy because of us."

I agreed and then asked her where she would feel safe. Josie just started to cry and I did not have any way to help her now for she knew that now she would have the weight of the world on her shoulders and no one to help her like, Rick or Charlie and even her ex-husband.

She knew I would help but she also knew that I had a mission of my own now and that was to find Charlie and make sure he does not do anything that will get him killed. I always have a hunch that Charlie entered the military for the only reason of finding Syeed and killing him. Now after what happened I feel he will move even faster to try and find him, anywhere that he is hiding. Syeed felt that without Rick his war would end very quickly, but he never knew that another person with a vengeance to see to it that he is eliminated and never more to do any harm to any person, is about to be hunting him no matter where he will be.

I told Josie that she should start to get ready soon to leave. I made a plan that she should get a few throw away cell phones to keep in touch with me and to let me know where they might settle down until she knew it was safe. Josie was to go to her bank in the morning and withdraw enough money for the two to travel and live for at least a month.

Her friend did offer his car for them to get away and not have any way to know what vehicle that they will be traveling in.

Josie looked at me and started to cry again and said, "Bob I thought that it was over and now again.

I am taking my family and running away from these bad people." I told her that if Charlie has his way it won't be long before it is over for good.

CHAPTER EIGHT

I woke up to a beautiful morning. The sun was coming up and a cool breeze on this hot day felt so good. Birds were singing and children were running and playing in the street. Josie and Terri were already packed up and told me to take my time that no one is a big hurry today to run away again. I told them that I truly hope that this will be over soon. I let them both know that Charlie now has a complete special operation unit with him on this journey that he has found himself on.

I again told Josie that he is the brains sort of speak of the unit. He decides where and when to attack and per him he has not been wrong very many times.

Josie then said to me, "to take care of myself and to do my best to find Charlie before he gets into too much trouble that even his unit cannot get him out of. She then said to just close the door that it will lock, but after you do a walk around the condominium to make sure everything is turned off."

I agreed and told them to be safe and give a text with the throw away phone when you find a haven.

I finished getting dressed and made sure everything was turned off and closed the door and as I walked down to my car that I rented, I wondered where will I find Charlie and mostly how will I find him. I got into the car and tried to plan to locate him but I just decided to wing it as usual.

I drove back to the cemetery and this time I hoped I would not have any disruptions when I knelt to talk to my friend. As I knelt in front of his gravestone I could only think of all the good that we did together. I said to the grave that I wished he was still here because I feel that Charlie is about to do something that will probably get him killed. I said that he has such a vengeance to have the person pay for your leaving us.

At that moment, the hair on the back of my neck was going up and I hoped that no one was here to harm me, because I have a very important mission now and that it was only your ghost Rick. I smirked at that thought.

I got up from the grave and gave a pat on the stone and then wondered why they had a grave for you since you were cremated. I guess it was because it was a family plot or something. After I patted the headstone for luck I again asked Rick to be there for Charlie and me, for I have a new mission and Charlie has a dark vengeance to follow.

As I started to leave the cemetery I still had such an uneasy feeling of a presence with me.

I looked up and said I do hope that it is you Rick and not anyone that we have killed together looking for their revenge today.

I got back into my vehicle and decided to try the Guard unit over by the park now; they set up just after the attacks and stayed since.

I felt that if Charlie needed any information of what was happening around here lately that the Guard was a place to start.

I was partially right, for Charlie did stop by and that he only wanted info and then he left with a group of bad asses one soldier said to me. I thought that at least he is very well protected right now. I do fear that he may just go rogue if his commander would not agree with his new mission.

After the unit at the park, I went to a small bar not far from the park. This was a place that a person like me would not go into alone. Well, that is exactly what I did and it was worth it. As I entered a voice came from the back of the room, and I went to it. Now I know how dumb I am right now but I needed some answers of where Charlie is going. I came to a table of men, or maybe gorillas. These guys were huge and all had a smile on their face. One asked me why I am looking for Charlie. I told him that I am kind of his uncle. He said kind of? I told him quickly that I was his Uncles traveling companion years ago.

One of the biggest men stood up and said that then you must be Bob. I reluctantly said yes I am. He and all the others stood up and saluted me.

I asked them why they did that and each one said that what Charlie has told us all, that you are a hero just as much as his Uncle Rick.

I thanked them all and then asked them where I could find Charlie. They all said that Charlie is now began to dance with the devil and hopefully will make it back soon. I asked them what they meant and one said that Charlie has a demon and today he starts to end its grasp over him.

I then sat down with these guys and ordered a scotch over ice, for I now feel it is what I need to continue the journey to find Charlie.

I continued to ask the men of his unit why are you here and Charlie is gone. One guy said that Charlie is a thinker and a finder. The commander figured that he should let him run loose for a short time before we come to where he is at. Another said that Charlie will be ok; you see he is a badass on his own. He stands around 6'2" and is not big but is solid as a rock. And his fighting skills are excellent. Plus, Charlie took his two gorillas with him, and they all laughed. I just looked lost, and one said that is what we call his two best friends. They are huge and probably clean this whole bar out and sit down for a beer without breaking a sweat. I was starting to feel a little better but not enough yet.

I asked them how long of a leash do you give him before you automatically go after him. They all said not too far, he must check in on a timely basis and if not we are off to his last position.

And at that moment entered a small man, compared to the others. He swayed into the bar with a high on himself attitude. He sat down next to me and said that if I can see him I can protect him. I turned to this guy and said then you are the shooter.

He nodded with some pride and then asked me who I was. I let him know that I am Charlie's Uncle Bob. He stood up and said I am Sergeant Jimmy, I mean James Smith. I looked at him standing at attention and then asked him why he was. He said Sir may I shake the hand that shook the hand of a true American Sniper, and a hero to all us shooters.

I then stood up and said that may I shake a hand of a hero that is with us right now. He smiled and said how proud he was to be able to help Charlie in his endeavor to kill Syeed.

I paused and let them all know that I knew he was going after someone but that you know the story of that day! Yes, sir said Jimmy and we know of the sacrifice that you gave to be with him on his mission that day. I told them that Rick James was the best friend that I could ever want and a true comrade in arms. I counted on him and him on me.

At that moment, they all asked me to go over that day so they can understand Charlie's demons. I did not want to bring back memories that I hoped on not remembering, but I did.

We stayed at the bar until it closed and I told them the story of that battle that I lost my friend and Charlie lost his uncle that he just found not long before it. All of them were so interested in what I was telling them.

Most of all was Jimmy, he was so amazed at what I told all of them and he kept shaking his head. I asked him why he was doing that, and he said that it was a shame that a man like Rick had his life ended so soon.

I then told him that Rick lost his life doing what he was trained for. It did not matter if it was overseas or next door, he did what was right and that was to protect his family and his country. They all gave a cheer and a toast to Rick.

The bartender was a little afraid to ask us to leave so he could close for the night but he did. And one by one they walked by him and gave him a very nice tip and left the bar.

I was so thankful that men like these here were part of Charlie's new family.

I went to my motel and went right to sleep for those guys made me wonder how to stand with all that drinking that we did. I woke up and after a shower and breakfast I decided to look up everything that of Charlie's plan.

I went to Charlie's office and when I entered I heard a gruff voice laugh, I could only imagine of what you all went through last night. This man sitting in Charlie's chair in his office wanted to know if his men had treated me well and gave me the type of welcome a person like me deserved. I again looked at him and wondered what he meant and then he said that, he was Rick James commanding officer back in Afghanistan. I almost fell with that statement, but I sat down.

I looked at him and said that Rick could not say enough good about him and that he felt that if it was not for you that he might be dead a long time ago.

The commander then told me that Rick was a one of a kind, he told me that if it was not for Rick that so many terrorists and plain old bad guys would still be around today. I gave him a nod and with that we both agreed he was a special person to his country and especially to us.

CHAPTER NINE

The commander asked me if I wanted to have dinner and he will give some more information about who Charlie Walters is now. I thanked him and we were off to a little restaurant just around the corner from the base. I told the commander that things are different here and in most places in this country after what went on. He knew all of what happened to Rick and me from the first journey until our last that ended in the park not far away.

When we arrive at the restaurant and we both took our seats, I asked him if Charlie told him about what happened at the cemetery the other day. The commander said that he knew that there was some type of commotion and that the boys handled it. I again asked did you know exactly what had happened, especially to Charlie's mother. He looked at me in bewilderment and said that they said a commotion not anything else. He then asked me what did happen, Bob. Because I feel that I now understand Charlie's new desire to go after...I stopped him and said Syeed. The commander just nodded and I did as well.

He said that he better tells me of some of Charlie's missions and that may give me an idea of where Charlie was going.

I knew that he was going after him ever since that day in the park when his uncle and I did battle with him. I then let him know what happen the other day in the park. I told him that we were at the grave site and Josie, his mother had a feeling and she turned to me, so she was sideways to the headstone at that moment. And at that exact instant a rifle fired and the bullet hit the bottle of beer that I put on Rick's headstone in his memory. The memory that in all the travels together that Rick and I never sat down and had a drink together, just relaxing and talking about anything but nothing. The commander said that he could feel the need to have that one special time together after all that you two have been through.

Then I told the commander that after the shot I heard noises up by a mausoleum on top of the hill, and Josie turned again and said that she knew the noise was from Charlie. She was right, because he was with two mountains and they chased down the shooter and his friend. Well, you have an idea how the two men ended up. He nodded yes and then said that those two mountains will and have taken a bullet for Charlie before and will do it again, the red headed one is Riley and the brown hair is Jack. They are the three musketeers and they let everyone know it. I asked what about the rest that I met in the bar.

He said that they are the advance team and they rely on Charlie for the correct information for the target and of course Jimmy, he just loves being a part of Charlie's team because of his admiration of his uncle being a great sniper.

Now Bob sit back and let me give you just a touch that I can tell you of Charlie in the military. When he first arrived at the base he did everything that he was told to do and worked harder than any other trying to make it as a sniper. Charlie had such a burning desire to be just like his uncle and be a sniper, and even with desire he also needed good eyes and a steady hand. He had neither because of his vision been not up to par, but most of all when Charlie tried to calm himself to make a shot that is when he became so nervous. Others tried to let him know that his eyes can be corrected, but his nerves cannot unless he learned to take that deep breath and let it out slowly then shoot. I think that he thought way too much on the breathing that he could not breathe.

After Charlie joined the unit Jimmy came to him because of what he heard of him trying to become a sniper and didn't, and told him that the world will not end because he could not make it. Then Jimmy found out who he was related to, that made him go back to Charlie and let him know that anytime you want, you want to be my spotter you can. Jimmy adored other past snipers always feeling that they were in a club that no other could be a part of. Charlie truly appreciated what Jimmy was doing but he told him that he didn't make it as a sniper but I am the best Finder.

And everyone in the unit agreed with him of the assumption that Charlie can locate anyone anywhere in the world. That is why they all respect and trust him.

But lately, I think that Charlie has his own mission and so do the others. They all feel that no matter what they will be there for him in whatever situation he gets himself into. I looked at the commander and asked him what is it that Charlie has devised to find Syeed. He looked back and said that only Charlie knows and that is how he has always put his missions together. He was the only one to know until the mission started.

You see he had a method that he would come up with that he could locate a person from his emails or text along with actual info from a human source. These sources that he has, have not been known by others, because of privacy and of anonymity of the source. Charlie developed a network of people that with just a one word or a text could put together an area where a person of interest was now at. In just plain English, Charlie was a genius of finding people. And find them he did, and with all the finds he never was satisfied with the target. I feel that with all he has known of all the people that he has gone after that he will never be satisfied with anyone else than Syeed.

With that statement, I agreed and thought to myself that he also can be killed by that same target, and not have revenged his uncle at the same time.

CHAPTER TEN

One mission that Charlie and his team went on was just inside of a town in Yemen. This place was absolutely a complete mess of a town that had more holes in the roads than Swiss cheese. But Charlie knew or felt, sometimes what no one else knew.

That the target we were after was now in that town and everyone around him did whatever it took to protect his presence in the area.

Charlie has a unique ability of locating people, all but Syeed so far. He will use emails from the area and text and phone calls, then he puts that information on sort of a spreadsheet and from there he will decide what part of a state city or region the target may be hiding in. So far, he has been over 90% correct.

On this mission in Yemen Charlie had it 100% and the target was even in the room that he felt that he would be on that exact day.

Charlie asked Jimmy if he could be there with him for the shot, Jimmy always gave into Charlie not only because of his uncle but he was a likable guy and everyone knew him and what he can do and that made things so much easier and quicker, and that is why Charlie was at the spot to watch and would have almost the same feeling as if he made the shot himself.

On this day that was to be a quick hit, but turned a touch bad for the unit. During the calculations that Charlie did he did not take in consideration that it was the beginning of the holy week. That through his spot off by approximately 100 or so yards in the next building, the group of people gathered in that building instead of the one that had thought them to be in. Charlie panicked after he caught the mistake but was too far away to yell out at Jimmy, and could not run to him fast enough, so he did the next best thing and ran to the right building and made his way to the room that the target was now in.

Charlie did not shoot anyone on his way up he just hit them to knock them out and knifed them.

And when he came almost to the door two guards were there and Charlie pulled out his pistol and proceeded to shoot his way into that room. The unit heard the gunfire and not seeing Charlie wondered what happened to him. They thought that he may have been spotted and was taking on fire from the targets men.

Then they realized that it was coming from the building next to the targets one, Jimmy said to the others that I think Charlie made a mistake and went to handle it on his own.

His two buddies Riley and Jack that were attached to watch him heard the gunfire and then noticed that Charlie was not behind them like he should have been. They ran towards the shots that they heard and started to climb the stairs up to the sounds. On the way, they saw men out cold and some stabbed, the two just shook their heads and wanted to smile but didn't.

When they made it to the room that had the door opened, they heard a voice saying that if you give me information on Syeed that I will then let you live. The other voice said something that was not speaking, must have had a mouthful of Charlie's fist, and then we heard another gunshot and Charlie walking out of the room. He looked at the two and said that I did give him a choice. Then they smiled now knowing that Charlie was safe.

Charlie was not happy as he walked down the stairs, he knew that one thing that he miscalculated the spot and the other was he did not get the information that he had hoped he would get from the target.

After Charlie went back to command, he first apologized to the others of his stupid mistake as he called it, and let them know that if he had caught it 10 minutes earlier that things would have been different.

Jimmy just looked at Charlie and said you wanted to have the notch on your belt from this hit. Charlie looked stunned and Jimmy just laughed at his expression.

But I was the one who was concerned at what just transpired and only hoped that it was a real misjudgment and not one that was on purpose so he could do what he did. I looked at the commander and said that I feel it was a little of both. I knew Charlie enough to know that he is a straight shooter and that he would never put any other person in danger.

And I think that after he found out that he made a mistake in location that he knowing he could not warn the others without giving all the positions away.

He did what comes naturally to his blood and went and handled the situation on his own. And I feel after he realized the error he also decided that this would be a good time to question the target before he was eliminated.

The commander looked at me and said that he felt the same way about the ordeal and that he only hopes that on this new mission that he does not have the same miscalculations as he did in Yemen.

CHAPTER ELEVEN

After a great time having dinner and talking about Charlie's adventures I thought that it was time to turn in. I asked the commander if he could give me an idea of where Charlie may be heading so I can try and get in front of him so he was not to put himself in harm's way because of passion and not what is right and safe. He told me that his mission is sanctioned and that it was classified. Then he said to me that have you ever been to Detroit? I gave him a wink and then thanked him for dinner and the stories.

As I walked back to my motel I could not stop thinking that Charlie is on a mission that will end in either Syeed's life or his. When I was in my room I opened my bottle of scotch and poured a lot over ice, I need to sleep good because tomorrow I head to Detroit.

I woke up around eight, that was later than I wanted to. And after I got up and was ready for this day that just began. I knew that I was to travel to the north and not know what was waiting for me or for Charlie.

I thought how much easier it would be if I could only call or radio him, but when on a mission no calls in or out from any else but the communication officer. That ensures complete safety of the operation and the people in it. If someone could communicate with them or them with someone on the outside another set of ears may not be too far away listening to the whole operation.

After a quick shower and a light breakfast, I was off on my hunt for a person, that was Charlie, and if I could get to Syeed first then that would be my opportunity to obtain my revenge that I have held in for so long on that man. I would never have denied Charlie from his but if I was there in front of him first then I know I would not be able to control my anger and desire to see that man fall from my hand.

I know Charlie will be careful in his new assignment to find this target in hopes of finding another and then another until he finds the one that he wants...Syeed. And Charlie has a large cheering section for him to accomplish what he has set out to do so many years ago, his family, mine and so many other people that was injured or killed by this man and his followers.

I went by the strike team's barracks to let them know that I was leaving and that I will be traveling up north too long way back to my home in Ohio, I said that I have not been through Detroit for a long time.

One looked up at me and said that Detroit could be a dangerous city if you end up in the wrong place.

I told them that I have an idea that I can just follow the bread crumbs to get to safety.

They laughed and told me that sometimes you should wait back until the area you want to go into is safe. I told them that I feel that when I get around to the area I want to be in I will feel the strike from above to clear my way. Jimmy just nodded and looked at me with compassion and at the same time pride, for what I am willing to endure to get close to Charlie, to be there in case he needs another friend. He has absolutely a completely prestige unit, to be with him when the time comes that they are needed, and two large friends with him right now on his undertaking, so why am I going, that reason is just like Charlie's and it is for my revenge too.

I left their area and headed up north for my next journey, but this time alone! I know that I am too old now to run and jump out of the way of danger if it comes fast at me, but I need to be part of Charlie's revenge.

And I promised his mother that I will get to him to help protect him and to ensure that he does not do any dumb mistakes or take any type of extreme measures to obtain his objective on this calling that he has started for himself.

As I was driving on the interstate leaving town I went back some time ago when Rick and I went on our journey's together to keep my promise to my family, and for Rick to keep a promise to himself to find and keep safe his family.

CHAPTER TWELVE

Today I travel alone to keep a promise to Josie, Terri, and myself to make sure that Charlie completes his mission and for him to make it back to his family safe.

I stopped at a rest stop just outside of Detroit. I was quick going in and out for I remembered all too well what happened at the stops that Rick and I stayed at. I then just pulled off the road and thought for a minute of in what direction I should go. I tried to get some information off the internet with my phone on the area. Yes! Me! With the phone finding things, Samantha showed this old guy how to use it in the way I needed today. She told me that she may be out of a cell tower range and I would not be able to get in touch with her if I needed information right away. I searched for areas around the city that has a new and concentrated immigrant population from the Middle East for starters. Since Syeed was from Afghanistan I felt that the most likely area would be of his countrymen and then I would expand my search after that to other similar spots first then move out to areas that have been established for a long time.

I think that if I was to hide in a new country, a country that was out for my head, then I would try to stay in an area that no one would expect a person like Syeed to stay without his main protection. I still feel that in that type of area there are many sympathizers of what he stands for so, I start with the worse area and work my way up.

The city that I picked out first was an hour away and on the way, many parts of town that you felt that you needed an AK47 and some blasters to get through, yes, I still call flash bang grenades, blasters. Just sounds so much more dangerous, flash bang grenades! Or BLASTERS!!!! Yes! Blasters! So on to the city of my first choice, and this city is not one of someone my look would be very welcomed in.

As I drove to my first of many I feel places to try and locate Charlie I tried to make some type of plan when I did get there and the only plan that kept going through my head was, wing it!

So, as I stopped just on the outskirts of town I notice that all the billboards and signs on store fronts were in a Middle Eastern script.

I took a very deep breath and entered the city limits, to only stop once when I noticed a shiny glimmer up on top of a building to my right. Was that just an object on the building that was giving off the light or a person with a scope, I was hoping for an object.

I just continued through the town since I was not about to stop and get a coffee in it. I kept a good eye all around me in hopes of a sign that Charlie was close.

I was about halfway through the city when I looked up at a billboard and on it was sprayed with paint, UB and an arrow pointing north. I almost did not believe it but Charlie knows that I am right behind him. I guess his buddies gave him heads up. UB uncle bob and an arrow pointing to the town that I knew would be the place for an arrogant bastard as is Syeed or even his loyal followers.

Now after I drove out of the city I have a feeling that the glimmer on the building was also a sign to me, from Jimmy. These guys are truly a bunch of fabulous special operation friends of mine now. When I was out of the city I noticed another painted sign on another billboard that just said, Made It! I almost ran off the road because I laughed so hard at that one. I think that Charlie knows I am coming.

The next town was approximately a half hour or so down the road I was on. I was always looking for another type of sign that the unit would give me. Now I know that Charlie is safe for he is with a magnificent group of men now. And, a woman is in the unit, because that is what the commander told me before I left to come here. She is a true special operations member; she does what is needed and is what was said a valuable partner to Charlie. When Charlie needs a person to bounce off his ideas, she is the backstop.

She is also a very qualified in being an interpreter and a technical expert, and that is what Charlie needs more sometimes than an army of guns.

Charlie told his group that if he had a choice going into hell with his unit armed to the teeth or with his most loyal technical person that he would pick Jenny.

He knew that between language knowledge she also knows of the entire internet, phone, and other items to help me figure out a scenario to either get out of a situation or to find the target plus knows how to use a weapon. And as one guy said that she is also hot, that helps her with Charlie I think also.

I feel that Charlie is too dedicated to his operation to let beauty interfere with what he wants with the outcome of it. Her being good looking I am sure is just a plus and nothing more, I think.

I was just about to enter the city limits of the next town when I saw my next sign from Charlie. I stopped dead in the middle of the road for up ahead was a woman in shorts, very short at that and legs that went to the sky. Black hair with green eyes is what I saw as I came up to her, and waving for me to stop.

I pulled over to the side of the road and rolled down the passenger window and asked her if I could help her.

She smiled and I mean a smile, she was a beautiful woman, too young for me but, wow! She then said that she was here to help me, and you had better open the door so I can get in or people will talk and she then laughed, I looked at her and ask Jenny? She smiled even bigger than before and said that Charlie told you of me, I said sorry but the commander did. She then said that at least someone recognizes me. I then said that you are hard not to recognize.

So why are you here if I may ask? She said that Charlie gave me orders to make sure that you make it safely to where he and his team are at. He knows that you have a demon in you just as he does of getting the man that took away his uncle and your friend. I then told her that I am too old to fight anymore and I feel that this vengeance is up to Charlie now. She shook her head and said that Charlie and others told me some of the adventures that his uncle and you have been through in your travels.

And, some of the dances, I laughed and told her that I still can't dance. She then being extremely serious said, but you still can shoot, right. I looked at her and said point to Syeed and I will show you how I can shoot. She smiled again and said then it is settled, we travel together.

CHAPTER THIRTEEN

Charlie was in the next city with his entire unit, he felt that he was on with who he wanted to get today and it wasn't Syeed, but one of his top people. And for Charlie right now that was enough. He gave a signal to Jimmy not to fire just yet, and he directed his two guards to go down and see if he has anymore guards than we can't see from here. Everyone did just as Charlie had ordered and no one complained at what he wanted, because they all knew that he is doing this to get the target and not for any other reason.

When his two front men went down to check the area out before any others would descend to street level in search of their target. Charlie already knew that he was in the building. He wanted to hopefully take him alive for to interrogate him on the whereabouts of Syeed. He instructed his men that if possible to take this one alive and if it meant harm to any one of our team the process of eliminating or capturing the target.

Jenny and I are too far away to participate in the mission that they are about to begin.

So, for now we are left out of it. Jenny looked at me and asked me if she could shake the hand of the man that danced so his uncle could make his shot because you were dancing to distract the shooters. And I said that I also was shot in the shoulder and got a brand-new truck for Rick and me to travel in. She laughed and wanted to know of who Charlie's Uncle Rick was. I told her that that man was the best friend and the most prepared and trusted military person that I have ever had the opportunity to know.

I then gave her a brief history of what Rick and I went through to get to my daughter and then to his sister and her family. Jenny was so astonished at what we did for each other and told me that she would do the same for Charlie. Now I knew that she meant more to him than just another person in his unit.

Charlie was confused at the information that he had just obtained from his sources, and wanted to know what was in store for his unit when he decided to attack. He knew that there was a high value target somewhere inside of the gated Community that they were sitting outside of. Charlie went over all the Intel and kept thinking if he was in the right spot for the hit or extraction of the target.

Charlie radioed Jimmy to ask him if he can see some type of movement other than the normal that would be happening around this area.

Jimmy called back and said that all seems to be beyond normal here. Charlie thought a second and said to himself, beyond normal?

He then radioed his two trusted point guards; he asked them if they see anything out of the normal around where they are positioned. They both called back and said just as Jimmy just told you, beyond normal. Charlie knew that this is an upscale community and that a good portion of the residence would not be around during the day for being at work or either could be out of town, but he kept thinking that something is not right here.

Jenny and I were still a little bit away from where the unit was at and she just said to me that she has a feeling and I think that it is not good. I asked her what she meant by that statement and she mentioned some of the scenario's that Charlie and she would go over to conclude where a target would be at. She said that I cannot get this thing out of my head of how easy it was to find these people here. I then spoke up and said can you radio Charlie and she smiled and nodded.

When Charlie heard from Jenny he immediately told all to pull back and that a problem may be right around us now. Jimmy said that he will stay in his position until everyone pulls back to the gas station on the corner. The others started to move back when the two guards radioed that they see movement and a lot of it.

They said that just about every garage door opened at the same time and what they can see now is vehicle pulling out of them and all have at least four inside of each.

Charlie now knew that this was a setup and that they all had better move quickly, He radioed to Jenny not to come and to the others that a fight is about to begin. They all called back and said to Charlie that they will be ready.

Up high in a spot that looks over the entire area was Jimmy and he was ready right now. He started to scan the vehicles for he did not want to hit a civilian vehicle. The two that were assigned to guard Charlie moved close to where he was at and the others all moved out in different directions and started to get ready.

Jenny was in a panic about what she felt was about to happen to the unit, and she feels that some of the blame was on her. She asked me to go faster so we can get there to help them. I told her that Charlie may feel they can handle what may come their way now and for us to be safe and stay back. Jenny then turned to me and said Bob please help me to help them. I considered her eyes and saw what I used to see in Rick's when he was in his military mode. I put my foot down harder on the gas pedal and we were on our way to who knows what type of trouble right now, I pulled out my 9mm and put it down on the seat next to me and Jenny was doing the Rick with her weapons.

I do miss him, especially at a time like this. She took out two 9mm's and a huge knife that she strapped to her leg, the two pistols she holstered and put two extra magazines in her belt. This woman was extremely ready and I for one do not want to be in her way when things get hot.

We were going as fast as I could go around this area and Jenny just stared out front of us. I told her not to worry that if needed I will dance again, she broke out in laughter and that made the rest of this ride bearable.

Back at the gated community that the team was at, Jimmy was up high and ready, Riley and Jack spread out to cover any advance that would come towards Charlie. The rest of the team split into two's and proceeded to cover all ways to them.

They did not ask why but followed what he wanted them to do. Riley and Jack would do whatever that Charlie wanted them to do for they trusted all his decisions so far, and he has never let any of the team down. Now Charlie feels that he has them right where he wants them right now.

As they came forward towards the team, Jack and Riley shot short burst to get them to move, Jimmy was smiling for he had every one of the vehicles and what men were out of them in his sights.

He thought that Charlie did it again.

We were seconds away and I thought that Jenny was going to burst, and I said to her that when we get closer that I will slow down to a crawl and that she should get out and move around closer to the action and make their day, she again laughed and said to me thank you and I hope I see you on the other side. As she got out of the car I thought aloud that I will be right by you, and that no one will die today.

Things started to get hot and Jimmy was, good shooting ducks in a barrel. His two downwind of him had suppressed fire until they all went to his right and the rest of the team did their job and eliminated most of them who have come this way.

Charlie was now surprised at their military action and started to rethink immediately, for now he feels a trap.

And he was right because a group came from their left and they were well armed and coming fast.

Charlie then felt that the team could not turn and take the fight back to that way when, Jenny and Bob came moving fast to the left of us and was taking out anyone in their way. This girl was amazing with sitting out the window and firing at the enemy. When I watched, her do what she did, I remembered Rick out of the sun roof doing almost the same. The only thing that I could get out was to save one for me, and she quickly turned and said then we better get there soon.

Just as we arrived and Charlie and his team fought off all the ones that they did, he then radioed to the others, what just happened. Jenny radioed now and asked the same of Charlie.

Charlie sat down on a large rock used for landscaping and said that he has out foxed me this time. As I came up and heard what he just said I asked him what he meant. Charlie said that these men were checking us out today, and sacrificing their men to find out what we know and how we fight.

Charlie said that we do not chase or follow because that is what they want us to do so we will wait and listen for their celebration of what they felt that they did to us, and then we will give them a surprise when we decide to.

Charlie said that he will have every asset out trying to listen to what they are up to and of hopefully the next move that they will make towards us or the next destination that they will be heading to.

CHAPTER FOURTEEN

The next day as we all awoke from what we all felt was a disaster; Charlie was smiling and told everyone how great they all did in letting the enemy feel that they had us. Riley and Jack just shook their heads in amazement of what Charlie just said. Charlie insisted that what happen to them yesterday was not all bad; he said that because of what and how they were doing different tactics it has given me the insight into who they have been possibly training with. And most importantly where!

Jenny now started to get what Charlie was now saying; she understood his analytical mind not like the rest of us, they only understood where and when and how to battle. That is why Charlie and she get along so well, they have a mind that thinks alike. Jenny and Charlie took off into their world and the rest of us into ours; I went up by Jimmy and thanked him for the sure shots that gave us cover as we were coming in.

He said that he only did what any other member of this unit would do. Again, I thanked him and he just nodded.

Riley and Jack were sitting across from each other and started to throw their knives at each other's feet, and what another told me was that they try and see who can get the closest without the other flinching. I said that these two are so unusual, and I said that I meant that in a nice way, I think. Jimmy came by me and said that, "if you have the chance to be in battle next to these to unusual guys, you will see why they challenge each other. Yesterday when things got hot, Charlie just looked at them and they already knew where to go to, and where Charlie was heading at the same time. They are in exact timing of each other and know any motion or direction that Charlie may have at any given time."

I looked at them and said that his Uncle Rick and I were getting into sync almost the same way, except without the throwing of the knives.

Charlie came up to me and asked me, "If I had fun yesterday," and Jenny turned in his direction and said, "Charlie! Do you really think that what happened yesterday was fun?" He looked down as if he was embarrassed, and I spoke up and said, that it would have been a little bit more fun if I could have thrown a few Blasters! Everyone just stopped what they were doing and asked me what a blaster is. I said that a Blaster! Is a flash bang grenade, I used to call to his uncle to throw a blaster or it is my turn to throw a blaster? When there is just the two of you and you do not ever know when your number has been picked, you need a diversion between each other just for the fun of it.

In one battle, I shot off fireworks to confuse the enemy and yes, it worked.

Jenny came over me and sat next to me, and gently put her arm on my shoulder and asked me in a soft non-comedic way, "Uncle Bob can you please show us the dance that you did to get the attention of the sniper so Charlie's uncle could shoot him." I told Jenny that I danced and yes, I got shot, but we got the two snipers and a brand-new truck. Jimmy looked at me with a smile and said to me, "that yes a new truck was definitely worth almost being killed." I turned to him and said at the time of the shooting, it was well worth the lives that I saved because I put mine in jeopardy to save a town. Everyone was silent and then I stood up and, gave them a look at my dance. Everyone broke out in laughter and one of the men said, with that dance why you aren't dead right now. I looked back at him and said that I was a bit younger and that I did have some moves. Again, laughter!

Charlie came to my rescue and let his entire unit know that his Uncle Rick told him some stories of their adventures together and that Bob with no training what so ever picked up all of Rick's signals, something like Riley and Jake does. Plus, that my uncle never had any fear of anyone getting him from his blind side. And even though at the last battle my uncle was gone, Bob was in intensive care for over two weeks and no one knew, not even the doctors if he would live.

He almost gave his life so Rick could be with his family that he did not know that he had, and that was my sister Terri and me along with my mother his sister Josie.

In my mind that is a true hero and one that deserves all the respect of this unit.

Everyone stood and applauded me and I got up and, well danced and they loved it. I told them that I will do what is asked of me just as you all do of yourselves and that when the time comes, no dancing, just BLASTERS! They all cheered at that, and said but first we should find some.

Everyone then went back to preparing for what was coming for all of them, and no one knew what that was, except Charlie and Jenny.

CHAPTER FIFTEEN

A few days later after the battle that they were in, the unit was in very good spirits and was waiting for Charlie to give them their new orders of where they will be heading. I went to Charlie to let him know that if by chance that he does not have the opportunity to eliminate Syeed, that it would be ok with me and I am sure that your Uncle Rick would agree with me on that. He looked at me and said, "that this was for not only Rick but for Terri and my mom plus you." Again, I told him that all of us would rather have you alive then get vengeance on Syeed by giving your life for it.

Charlie looked at me, and this time with the Rick military look, he said, "that no matter what he had to do to avenge Uncle Rick, that he will do or give so it will be done."

What else could I do but nod in agreement, for to try and change his mind would only draw him deeper into the demons will.

I then told Charlie that I was going to go back to St. Louis and check the condominium and the entire area out for any trouble that may have stuck around just in case Josie and Terri came back.

After that, I will take back the rental car, and only hope that they will not be to mad at the bullet holes. Charlie smiled at that, and asked what then.

I told him that I am going to fly to my daughter in New Jersey and check on her and make sure that her mother is doing ok also.

He told me to not to worry so much because as you have seen I do have a very good support group around me. At that I had to agree with, that would have been great to have when Rick and I went on our journeys together. Then he may still be with us today.

I went around the unit to say goodbye and to wish them all well in all their endeavors that they will be in soon. They all said that I was welcomed to join the unit anytime that I want to.

I nodded and got into my car and slowly drove away thinking of Charlie and only hoping that he will be safe and get back to his family alive.

I drove straight through to St Louis and did not stop at any spots that looked like a good area to attack others.

I did not want any trouble anymore now that I know that Charlie is so far ok, and that with Josie and Terri in hiding for now, I just wanted some peace and quiet while I drove. I had the radio on to some nice smooth jazz and was feeling the beat. I tried not to think of anything that is bad but only that is good, things like my family and what I did just before I came on this new journey.

I have been driving for many hours on this long straight road and the great music gave be a moment of peace, but not for long. Just as I was entering the city limits I saw smoke coming from close to the area where Josie's condominium would be.

I drove cautiously now and turned the radio to a news station that I remembered from the last time I was here.

Just a small condominium fire and not much details about it, the newscaster kept saying that they were unable to get too close and that the fire department and police along with the State Troopers which she said was odd for an ordinary house fire.

At that moment, I knew that this as not just any fire and I moved faster to get by the units that I felt was on fire and to get as close to the police line as I could so I would hopefully be able to get close enough to see what was happening there.

When I was as close as I could go too, I got out of the car and walked up to the police line.

As I walked to the condo's I could smell the wood that was burning along with the odor of burning plastic, at that moment I could also smell the odor of gun powder and then was sure it was not an accident and was wondering how it happened and from what type of explosive that went off.

Just when I was right by the police line I looked over at the units and knew that it was Josie's that went up first. An officer came up to me and said that it was a good thing that no one was home when this happened, right Bob?

I turned to see two officers who I truly do not remember ever meeting, but did seem to know me. I excused myself and said that I am sorry but do I know you two. And one said that we met at the park on that day, and we were the two that brought you to the hospital.

I immediately thanked them both and shook their hands, and said to them on that day I lost my friend and we lost the target. One officer gave his condolences to me for Rick and said that you two truly did some massive damage on those guys before; well you could not fight anymore. The other said that when we arrived there must have been a hundred coming at you still even though it looks like a hundred were on the ground from you two. And when we all arrived we added to that number for sure. He then told me of the thoughts that every person had for the two of you sacrificing your lives for not only family but for the town.

I told them that I am sorry that I was not awake to thank you all then, but I did not wake up for almost two weeks and then I heard of Rick not making it and I went back into a coma for another day or so. The one officer said that they wanted, the town that is wanted to have a great big ceremony for him but his girlfriend took over because of his family was so distraught by the whole thing. She had him cremated right away and with just a small ceremony after then buried the urn in a plot that was bought by the town.

And she told everyone that Rick had a letter on him telling whoever, that he wanted to be cremated quickly and not to deal with his leaving his family, so for them to not have to grieve very much and for too long.

I told these two officers that at the time I was mad and then very happy that he was in peace finally. They nodded and then I said back to business gentlemen, what went on here and can you get me get closer.

While we were about to go under the tape stretched across the road a newscaster from the local television station asked why him and not the media. She then said that I want to know what happened here just as you do. One officer turned to her and was just about to speak when I said that I am a relative and am here to see what happened since the owner is away. She then said that the owner is Josie Walker and her brother and some other guy shot up the town years ago.

Many people were killed and they just disappeared from here and left all those dead bodies. I asked do you know who those bodies were and why they were killed that day. She just with a smug look said that they were men just in the park that day.

I said three hundred of them, and what were they there for, a picnic. They had their family and an AK47 rifle and as people walked by them they suddenly decided to shoot at them. She looked at me and said but they were human beings, and I said so was the rest of the people that died at their hand.

The two officers now saw that I was getting extremely irritated by this person so they started to move me away from her and just then Major Jones of the Guard came up to me and said Bob, great to see you all healthy now. It took a second but him I do remember because he sent the men to protect the condominium when Rick and I went to OKC.

The news lady then pushed her way to us and said that you are one of the two that did all the killing, and put this whole town on edge for no reason.

I had enough then and said to her that when that happened you were all of 12 or 13 years old and had no idea of what was going on in the country at that time. And that the men and yes woman came to our country to kill all of us not just some. In school, what did they talk about that makes you think that Rick and I were the bad guys?

She said our instructors told us that those people came in peace and the militant people of this country did not want them here. I just wanted to meet this teacher and teach him or her, a very valuable lesson of what life is all about, and that is not sitting in your office reading of what it should be like instead of what it was like. I tried to tell her that Rick died to save his family and this town and that I was in the hospital for weeks recovering from that battle, from the attackers, did you understand those words, attackers. They attacked and wanted to kill every American in this country and people like Rick and I plus men like these two officers defended your rights of freedom and you're right to live.

But you have no real idea of what went on only that some nut case professor told you that we were bad.

Now I need to know how the terrorists blew up Josie's condominium. She gasped and said you said terrorist? And I said I feel it may be terrorists and at that moment with her being in total confusion I went to the condominium and needed to see how they blew it up. When I arrived one man from the bomb unit said that it was not a bomb but an RPG that hit this unit and the one two doors down. I thought Stacy's unit. But she has been gone from it for years, so they have not been around here for some time, I think they are just giving a warning now.

I told all that was there that I would appreciate all information of what happened here to be sent to Charlie Walters, son of the homeowner.

CHAPTER SIXTEEN

I watched as the fire department put out the fires completely, and made sure that no one was inside. I was so mad at what happened but also happy that no one was injured, and that Josie and Terri were somewhere safe right now. I went back to my car and took out the note with one of the five numbers that Josie had on her five burner phones with her. I called it and after a few rings I heard hello! Josie this is Bob, did you hear anything about a fire at your condominium complex today, she said, "and it wasn't the complex it was mine and Stacey's units that were hit with some type of missile grenade.

Well, they tried at the cemetery and now they are letting us know where we live. She asked me of Charlie, and how was he doing now." I told her that he is doing fine; you know you have an unbelievable son in that man, and his unit is remarkable. They protect him as if he was gold, and Jenny does everything that is needed to help him. Jenny? Asked Josie!

I gave a little laugh and told her, yes Jenny is Charlie's assistant that helps him with planning and interprets for him.

And if I may be so bold she is attached to his hip, with her blue eyes and blond hair and complete athletic body. Josie then gave a smirk over the phone, and said, "like uncle like nephew."

She then said, "that so he is doing all right and is safe?" I told her that no one will be safe until your son finds and eliminates his demon. She asked what demon? And I told her that the demon that possesses your son every day and not until he gets him will he be freed. She gave a sigh and told me to do what I can to help him get this demon out of him soon.

I told Josie that I was going to my daughter and by her mother to make sure that they are doing ok and then I will hook up with Charlie where he might be at or heading to. She thanked me and told me to be safe also, and to not take any unnecessary risks when you find Syeed. I told her that if we come upon him that Charlie's unit will put one hell of a hurt on that man.

She laughed and told me to stay in touch. I agreed and we both hung up. And she threw away the phone that she just used. So, that no one would be able to trace that call.

After I finished the call with Josie, I called Sienna my daughter's mother and wanted to know from her if anything seems strange around her area. "She told me the only thing that was different was that a really nice couple moved into the house next door yesterday. She said that I did not know that the house was for sale or rent."

I asked her if she has talked to these nice people yet, only hoping that they were just ordinary people and not ones sent from Syeed.

Sienna then said, "Bob you sound worried? I thought that you sent the CIA to my area for some reason."

I said CIA? "She said yes Bob, they came by and introduce themselves and let me know that they will stay by me until the problem has been taken care of."

You didn't send them was the next question she asked me and I was just as flabbergasted as she was right now. I began to tell her of what has happened in St. Louis and why I am calling when she broke into my speech with, "Samantha! Is she ok!" I told her that I am going to call her next and then take the next plane to her. She said that when she called here just this morning that nothing seemed to be wrong by her place. I told Sienna that the second I am with her I will call and after that make sure nothing goes wrong by her area.

I called Samantha and when she answered I just came right out with, is anything wrong or different by you right now?

"She said dad please keep your cool, and I will tell you all that has gone on around here since you sent the two gorillas that are here to watch me until you get here." I almost died when she said that and I then realized when she mentioned gorillas, that I just may know them.

I said to Samantha, would these two gorillas be called Riley and Jake? "She said, of course that is their names dad, they said you were just together in Detroit the other day."

I told her yes, we were and that I had no idea that they would be with you up in New Jersey.

I told her that nothing will happen with those two watching you. "She said dad they sit across from each other and throw knives at their feet and laugh."

I told her that the way they get ready is to make sure that they trust each other completely.

I then asked her was any other people around her area lately? "She said no bad guys if that is what you mean, just Charlie." I almost swallowed my tongue with what she just said to me. I said Charlie! "And she just said to me that yes dad and what a hunk, if Jenny wasn't here, who knows."

I said that Jenny is with him and she said, "that you can't pry the two apart." I also wanted to know who else and she just said, "that whole unit is here and they will leave as soon as you arrive here." I then asked her if Charlie mentioned why they were at your place today, and why two CIA agents just moved into the house next door to your mother today. Samantha laughed and said, "that dad really after all that we went through together, do you really feel that I am worried when Charlie and an army shows up by me.

Dad be careful and hurry to me, I know you want to be part of the hunt, but leave that to the younger ones this time."

I told her that I was just about to get a ticket to her and that I should be with her soon. I also asked her if the guys mentioned any place that they may be at or have the next spot that they will be. Charlie said that you will not know of it and for you to stay with me now. He said that this time it is his fight! Under my breath, I said no way is it his fight alone.

Samantha heard and let me know that I was needed with her and not running around the world looking for a ghost.

After I heard what she said I knew that the team will soon be going over sea, and now I had better hurry and get my passport up to date. I then told Samantha that I will be there soon.

I took the first plane to her and after I arrived at her apartment I looked around for Charlie. Samantha let me know that they were somewhere around her place, because they did like the dinner I took them to when they first arrived here. And that is probably where they are at now. I put my bags down and was immediately surrounded by the entire unit. I laughed and said that you know that all of you are so lucky that I know who you are. Jenny came up to me and gave me a hug, she smiled and said "that you know Bob that you would have been dead before you entered the apartment," and I said is Jimmy here?

Samantha asked who is Jimmy. And Jenny said that you never know where Jimmy is. "Samantha then said like Rick, who would appear when you needed him. And be sure that you were always safe!"

Jimmy came up to Samantha and said, "I could never be like Rick, for there is not another like that man." She smiled at Jimmy and said, "he was or is the best protector that I have ever known, next to my dad of course." I asked what she meant by when she talked about Rick, and she said is, and she said, "that he will never be gone in my heart. "

Jimmy put his arm around Samantha and let her know that nothing will ever happen to her if her father and he was close to her. She smiled and I gave Jimmy a look.

He looked back and patted his rifle and I patted my pistol. And we both laughed, and smiled at the fact that Jimmy had a thing for Samantha.

Samantha was 30 now and Jimmy was 32, so it made sense that they would be attracted to each other. But attracted is all I wanted right now until all this danger is over and some people could return to some type of a normal life.

I didn't want my daughter to feel a loss that others have in war, and for her to plan a future only to possible have that future end before it would get started.

I put that thought out of my mind for now and went to Charlie and asked him why his entire unit was here with my daughter hundreds of miles away from where you were just a day ago. Charlie looked at me and said, "not to worry but a group was spotted not far from here, and we were not sure if they were heading this way or another place. So, we or I decided that here is our best place to be just in case that here is where they are headed." I looked and said do you have any idea where they are right now? Charlie said, "somewhere in New York City and we have already notified the authorities of their existence in the city so they can watch them, so nothing happens and no one gets hurt."

I asked Charlie that couldn't this just be some type of ploy to gather more information on your unit and where and who you are. "And he said that I truly hope so!"

"You see I feel that we are being followed all the time, but right now I cannot make out who they are and what type of communications that they have." He also told me that don't worry about your daughter because I already have in place a unit of the undercover FBI watching her every move of where she goes to and any new person that may approach her.

I said that I do not feel that much better but, that what is being done is more than I could have asked for. Thanks, Charlie! He just nodded and I looked at Samantha and she smiled and said "not to worry dad, I will be safe and why don't you just stay with me so you are also."

I looked at her and the group and said for a while, but I have my demons also, and I need to get them out of my mind to have peace. Charlie smiled and said "stay Bob your daughter needs you and I will take care of our demons, very soon I hope. Bob for what I need is information of who is following us and why, also while we are having people looking at our every move, I have some very deep black ops following us to try and find out who is behind us, they are called the ghost squad and for a good reason, you never know where they are and when they will attack. Just a case of cat and mouse for now and soon

I should have the information that I need to locate Syeed and end this mission forever."

I pulled Charlie to the side so I could talk to him in private, because I am about to let him know of what happened in his mother's condominium and that she is safe. I said to Charlie a few days ago, someone shot RPG's into your mothers and Stacey's condos, I feel as a warning to leave them alone or else.

He smiled and told me that yes, he knew about the incident at her home and that she is safe where she is at. I looked at him and asked him if he knew where she was and he smiled and said "that is what I do, is to find people who don't want to be found. She is safe and without her knowledge she is being watched by federal agents that are undercover, just like Samantha and her mother.

By the way, your family back in Ohio, they are under watch by authorities there.

So, you take care of yourself and daughter and let me take care of our demon." I nodded and gave him a hug in thanks.

CHAPTER SEVENTEEN

A few days after they left for who knows where I was getting awful uneasy sitting around, even though I am doing things with my daughter and some others that I met by her, like undercover agents that I ran into, and I do mean ran into one of the deep black ops that were shadowing Charlie's unit.

I was walking to the diner not far from her apartment and as I turned the corner we smacked right into each other.

I had no idea who he was until he touched his ear that had a radio and receiver in it, and spoke to Charlie about what just happened to part of his team just a minute ago.

He grabbed my arm and told me to get to your daughter and get her to these co-ordinances and you should be safe. Then this man continued to talk to Charlie about the confrontation they had with a very large group of insurgents that must have been laying low all these years until they were put back into the search for all the people and families that were part of Rick James sphere of influence back then.

Charlie said that they broke off from him to watch a small group of men and women that they have been hoping that they would lead us to the leader or at least some higher ups.

When we were just outside of a small motel not far from here, we encountered a few men that just happened to come by the spot we have been for a few days. One of them got so lucky by noticing a quick glimmer from a metal piece that one of us moved by accident in trying to get in a position of defense in case we were spotted.

Well, let me tell you, in a matter of minutes at least 50 to 60 came out of all the doors in the motel. I gave the order to get out and said that we will find them later, on our terms, we were out gunned and had to fight to get out. Two of my men were shot and one injured bad and the other just winged, so we grabbed our wounded and took off as fast as we could move. We split up my unit which has six, and two went with the injured and two of us stood our ground to give time for the others to get away.

As soon as we felt that they had a good lead to get away from the battle, the other man and I split up and took off in different directions to get away. That is how I ended up running into Bob. He continued to talk to Charlie about who he felt was in that motel besides soldiers. As he was walking towards his hide out, I was with him step for step.

He turned to me and said I thought I told you to get your daughter and go to the place I gave you info on.

I then boldly, knowing who this guy is and how he could probably kill me in a hundred different ways, told him that aren't their six undercover agents watching her right now, and can't they get her to your site.

He stopped and said, "that you and Charlie have the same demon, don't you?" I told him yes, I do and I will not have any peace until that man is dead.

As we were walking together he kept telling Charlie what he saw and he then said, Charlie do you remember the man who was by Syeed's side during the video clip that was sent to all the stations when they attacked us years ago, Charlie said I was young and did not pay attention to most of the news, but that face I do remember because he kept pointing at the camera and saying that all Americans will die today. You could almost hear Charlie gasp over the com after he said that to him. Charlie just said aloud that it was Aziz, the man that after Rick was put to rest sometime later took a video of him dancing on his grave and laughing.

Charlie told the soldier to wait and his unit is on their way to meet up and that he wants this man alive so he can talk to him and after that, well what happens to him happens.

I could tell a sense of revenge in his voice, and I could not agree more of what he said but I told him that if possible can that decision be mine how he leaves us. Charlie came across loud and clear, yes!

I called Samantha and told her to go with the authorities and that I should be close behind her.

Which in my head was a lie; I had no intention to stop my search for any relief of my demons. And I had no idea of what this Aziz did, and I am going to dance on his corpse soon. At that moment, I felt just as I did when I was traveling around the country with Rick years ago. And that feeling is so good right now.

CHAPTER EIGHTEEN

When we all arrived at the safe site, I asked the leader who is this Aziz and what does he have to do with Syeed? "He said that he is his other brother, and that they both have their vengeance with Rick, because he was the shooter that killed his brother and that Aziz vowed to find him and kill him and anyone that he loved." So, it is not Syeed, but that it is Aziz that is doing all this mayhem.

And then I asked, "who knew that it was Rick, and who told them." He said, "that after your battle with Rick the news outlets flooded the air waves with pictures and all the information that anyone would need to find his friends and relatives."

I quickly checked with my daughter's protection agents to see if she was all right and that if any problems have come up in her travels to the safe house that she is now at.

She told me that everything is ok and that she is not afraid at this moment and that she does hope it will finally end soon.

I asked one of the men that I was with from Charlie's special ops unit that were tailing his unit, "does Aziz being here and causing trouble mean that Syeed is nowhere to be found in this country."

He said, "that Charlie does feel that he may not be here but that he is somewhere in the Middle East right now."

I thought that it must be that Aziz being family of Mohammed, and Syeed, he is the point man and hit man as it might be for the family.

I told the soldier that I want to speak to Charlie or Jenny, "because I need to know how much danger is in store for my daughter and her mother, along with my family in Ohio." He agreed and said, "that he will be here in a few hours and then we all can get our information together and see what direction that we will be heading in next."

I sat down and was trying to think of all that my family has been through, mainly lately because of my actions when all this carnage happened and Rick and I went on our journey's together.

But I know that nothing would change now because of the men that want revenge from us because of what Rick have done to their family. And because of all that we did to their people who attacked our country, they don't care that we defended ourselves, but only that we killed them.

So, they want revenge for something that they started and what disastrous battles they killed our friends and family in. In their minds, it was the will of Allah that gave them the right to kill and that we were not allowed to defend our life's, for to them we were not worthy of living.

I sat under a tree by a barn that they are using for their safe house; it is located just outside of town on a large farm with a lot of land around.

The barn is what you would call a dump but that is all they need to hide out until they all regroup with Charlie, then head out again to try and locate the insurgents, and try and find out where Aziz is now, and with getting him he will finally have the ability, to finally get to Syeed.

It was later in the day but still warm, but with a nice breeze blowing around. With all the land and no buildings, it had nothing to stop that breeze from blowing. I see now why they picked this place, because as far as you can see with your own eyes there was absolutely nothing in sight. Not any houses or sheds, or even animals roaming around the pasture. Very well set up here.

It wasn't an hour later after I was getting comfortable leaning against a tree, Charlie and his unit slowly started to wander into the perimeter around the barn. They came from every direction for not to make any type of grand entrance all at once.

Coming in by the dirt road behind the barn were Charlie and Jenny, along with Riley in front and Jake right behind them both watching every direction as they approached the barn, more came in and as I got up to greet some of them I asked, "where is Jimmy I did not see him come in."

And Charlie said, "you will not see him until we are all in and safe, he is not far away and probably looking at you right now Bob through his scope."

I looked around and just waved in hopes that he saw me and then I saw a clump of weeds walking up to me, and he said do you always wave at nothing and then he laughed.

I smacked him on the shoulder and said only was trying to be nice. He smiled again and I did also. He is one to have as a friend just like Rick was. When Jimmy took all his camouflage off, I had him sit next to me and asked him how he was feeling of this operation and if he thinks we have any chance in finding either Syeed or his relative Aziz. He shrugged his shoulders and said, "that Charlie is rarely wrong and that he feels with some minor adjustments he will get back on track of them."

CHAPTER NINETEEN

After we all rested a bit Charlie came out from his makeshift office and sat in the middle of our group, yes, I now feel I am a part of it, for how much longer that is up to Charlie. As usual, Jenny was right on top of Charlie listening to his every word and giving her two cents only when asked for by Charlie. But she was absolutely one of the most important people in this unit and Charlie and the rest knew it.

And after our first meeting I can also agree that she is well worth her and my weight in gold or any other thing that may be valuable.

Charlie started with wow! Did they give us a punch! Then continued with but, that also gave us so much information that we did not have before this day. I feel that more is going on here and that they must have some type of hit list of those who thwarted their campaign so many years ago.

I have informants all around the world and the only information coming my way from them is that they want my mother and sister and of course and me dead, also this old guy as they describe him that used fireworks to stop one of the advances on them. I had to laugh at the statement that Charlie just told us and that of me.

They are going after others in the military and law enforcement agencies; this is not being an all-out attack like years ago, but a pin pointed direct strike at certain people. And Aziz is the point man for this whole endeavor of Syeed's and that the big guy is in hiding and others close to him are not talking of his where about.

Charlie said that he feels he is in the Middle East somewhere and that he feels this man's ego will not let him stay hiding for long, if we get Aziz.

And if by chance we get him and he stays alive then that means he will come out and travel here to save him or to sacrifice him to revenge his brother Mohammad.

Like as if I was in school I raised my hand to ask Charlie a question, he looked at me and along with him everyone else could not hold back the laughter, and I then said my question "will my family be in danger or just me?" Charlie said that what he can hear is that they have no idea of your Ohio family and that your daughter and her mother, he is not sure about.

So, I again asked him "if my daughter and her mother need to go into hiding for the good I did many years ago, and because that someone feels I need to suffer for my deeds, by harming them?"

He then said 'that they will be well protected, until we can eliminate all the threats that we face this time." I shook my head and told the whole group that I was with; that we must do everything that is possible in our power to do just that and to make sure that everyone, not only our friends and family will be safe again, but that every person in this country will also be. I said to them, that it is now up to us to make America safe again.

Charlie stood up and said "the same thing and added that we all will not fail, and he vowed to have the people's life all be back together as it was previously. He then said that his new plan has some danger and some bait," everyone looked at him and said, bait? He then looked at me and said, "Uncle Bob can you get you're dancing shoes on one more time." I smiled and said, just call me bait! Charlie smiled and told me that he will let me know what he wants me to do and how to do it.

Jimmy came by me and asked me what Charlie just meant by your dancing shoes. I told him that when his Uncle Rick and I traveled to find Charlie's mom, we stopped in a city in upstate New York.

They were being held practically hostage by a sniper, and when we came through we stopped and gave a hand.

I was to spot for Rick, until he said he needed them to make some type of movement to find their location so he could take his shot.

He then told me that I should get up and dance a little to see if they take the bait, well they did and Rick shot both the sniper and the spotter, and I also got hit by the sniper, because he must have taken his shot at the same time Rick fired and well, through and through as the doctor told me.

I danced and Rick shot and we saved the town from that annoyance. Rick also got a great hunting rifle with a scope, and we also were given a brand-new truck for our troubles.

So not only did we get the bad guys but we got the satisfaction of killing two more of the insurgents that day. So now I feel that I had better make peace with my family, for soon I may be walking in the clouds with Rick, and the two of us can finally have that beer together that we never had a chance to have.

CHAPTER TWENTY

The next day just after I opened my eyes, I felt that when I get up I will be back six years ago, on July 4th smelling the brewing of coffee and hearing people talking and laughing, dogs barking and hearing Rick running and yelling at Helen to wait, and he will park her car for her as he always did. I would be walking through my apartment looking at all the pictures that I have of my daughter, as she was riding a horse in one of the many shows that she would be in. I would be pulling up the blinds to pear out the window at all the morning activity that was going on in the common area as the morning sun just started to rise in the sky.

My eyes opened and reality happened and what I saw was not the people having fun, but that of a group of highly trained military personnel, cleaning and checking their weapons to be ready for the next battle, one for sure that they all know will not be too far away from now. After I awoke I went right to my phone to go down my list and call my family and Josie and Terri. I first started with my Ohio family and Samantha's sister, they were all happy and doing fine, not a problem at all.

My sister being the one that worries for everyone else, asked me why the call, she saw through the glee in my voice. "She then said that she will not say a word to the other ones in the family and again wanted to know why I called." I then told her I am going after the ones that got Rick and have caused so much ugliness in our country and that if I come home that I am owed a nice dinner from her, she laughed and said, "that I will owe them all a dinner at a restaurant of their choice." I laughed back and said that I would go broke, and she said well, "then you will not leave again."

I finished the call with that I truly cared for them all and that I will do what I can to get back and take everyone out to dinner and all of us have the time of our lives. She coughed and I knew that she was about to cry, so I said goodbye and hung up.

Next I called Sienna, Samantha's mother and when I was just starting to say hello, she went on a rage of why I should go after those demons and why I am about to leave my daughter. I said excuse me but why are you saying that, and she said that her protectors told her that you are going after the demons that have invaded your head and that you are the bait.

I had no words for what she just said, so I said "that I was going to visit Josie and I have no idea what she got that information."

She again raised her voice and said, "that she knows the plan that Charlie gave her a head up so that she would have to do now to make sure that all of my family is safe for once and for and all."

I told her exactly what was going on with me being the bait to draw out the ones that we need to get to, and that even if I do not make it out of this ordeal that I do love all my family, and I want you to be the person to let them all know. I heard a gasp from her on the phone and knew even with that, she will make sure that all my family will know how I feel. I then said that I am going to call Samantha and tell her the truth also. "She agreed and wanted to let me know that what I am doing is really a good thing and that if, she again said if, something bad happens to me that she will let all know how I felt."

I told her that I know that all will be good and that I will be here to talk to everyone when it is over, and that things will be back to normal. She signed and said that the only thing that matters is that you are safe.

I called Samantha and asked her if she felt safe where she was staying for now, and if she would rather go to her mother's instead. Samantha told me that she will stay put for now and then asked me how long I feel this will go on. I told her that hopefully things will get better, Charlie has a plan and with any luck and it works, we will be together again and safe.

Her voice crackled now and she paused before her next comment, and it was why you must go with them and put your life in danger once more. I told her that what she just said is why, once more! And I believe it will be the last, either way it may end. I said goodbye and again promised to return.

Next I called Josie on our burner phone, and when she answered the call, I got a bad feeling of her hello. She didn't say hello in any type of a normal sound, but she said hey Bob what is happening, we are doing just great, we are around a bunch of friends and will be going soon to another place that they want to go to. And after we are there I will try to call or just wait for you. I knew that what just transpired was that of letting me know that she was in trouble right now, and she was letting me know that.

I quickly made my way to the communications officer and told him to trace this call if he could, he looked and said will do. Charlie saw fear in my face from across the room and ran over and quietly wanted to know what was wrong. He asked is it Samantha? I nodded no, and then the communication officer said to have it and I continued the call with Josie. I told her that we are doing fine and should reach our next destination within hours; she said that would be great if she could be with us now. I told her that we all will be together as soon as this is over and you will be reunited with your son, Charlie. I heard a sign of relief coming from her voice and she said that it is a shame that he is so far away now, and I said that he is in your heart and soon in your arms.

The call abruptly ended and Charlie turned to the communications officer and asked him, where are they? He said just outside of St. Louis, and I said to Charlie that she never left the area. He said that she went as far as OKC and I guess she then turned around to head back to be around an area that she was familiar with.

OKC was the last I had her and my sister at, and now she is back home and trouble found her, and we are on our way to find her before she disappears from us. And this time it may be for good.

Charlie looked at everyone and said, well I think my plans have just changed and we have a new mission now. They all let Charlie know that they all are with him and that they will do what is needed to help him get his family back and to have them safe again. Jenny came up to Charlie and gave him a hug and said to him the next woman to hug you will be your mother and sister, I promise. And with this new news I told Charlie that only a part of his plan has changed for now.

Charlie looked at me funny and said Bob; "you do understand that we are going to find my family, right." I said yes and we can do the part of your plan that draws out Aziz at the same time. He will not think that you are coming for your family if I am brought out for bait. He will be drawn to where I am at, feeling that you are close by putting a trap for him, using me as bait of course.

And that is almost what we will be doing besides redirecting his forces away from watching your family.

Charlie smiled and said you still have it Uncle Bob, and I said doing just what I feel your Uncle Rick would do in the same situation.

The hard part of this plan is how do we inform him of my where about and what if they bring your mother and Terri with them to use as their own bait.

Jenny spoke first and let us know of the vast media that is at the disposal of the military and of one such newscaster that just so happens to be, my sister. Charlie smiled and said to Jenny, now that is the reason that I love you so much, you are always one step ahead of everyone.

Jenny smiled at Charlie, but I know it wasn't for him talking about her intelligence, but those three words that came out of his mouth.

So, while Jenny tried to get in touch with her sister and Charlie began developing his new plan, the rest of the team continued in preparing for what was to come next.

Jimmy sat down next to me and said that what you are about to do for Charlie and his family is outstanding. I said to Jimmy that I am doing this to hopefully end the terror that is being brought to all our families today.

Jimmy then let me know that when you feel you are all alone in front of Aziz or just standing in the middle of nowhere, that I will have my scope on you and those around you that want to harm you.

I thanked him and told him that I always had the feeling of someone close by that would be able to help me out of a bad situation and eliminate any danger that was not far away from me, that would cause injury to me, and that person was a sniper like you, Charlie's Uncle Rick. He smiled and agreed with what I just said and he then got up and moved away.

I now know that someone sent these men and woman to me so that I can accomplish, possibly the last mission that I will be on. If I complete it and make it back alive to my family.

CHAPTER TWENTY-ONE

Jenny was with her sister explaining what they needed her to do and why, that part gave her sister an uneasy feeling of what she was attempting to accomplish by her breaking news, that of the story of where one of the many people that thwarted so many attempts by the terrorist to complete their wave of terror throughout the country years ago. Where has he been, and what has he been doing since he and another man traveled around the country to keep two promises and completing both, but not before killing hundreds of insurgents that were in their path to do just that.

Lois who is Jenny's sister knew that on its own it was a good human interest story, but what she did not like is that someone will die because of what she is going to do. She only hoped that her sister would not be one of those to die that day. She knew exactly what I was about to give up to save her friends and Charlie's family.

As Lois and I talked over some of the key points that I wanted people to hear and for there to have a certain amount of time for me to talk freely, for that is when I will call out Aziz.

That is when Lois asked me why are you about to possibly give up your life to get this man out in the open. And I told her that he is the first step to find the main one behind all the attacks then and now, Syeed! his older brother.

And I am going to put my life's well-being in your sister's team hands and most of all, the eye in the sky and its man on the ground with his scope. She just looked at me as if I was talking in fables now.

What I meant I said is that way up will be a drone with capabilities to see all around and with heat seeking capabilities to look inside buildings for any enemy that may be close to me. And the scope is Jimmy, he is my guardian angel on this mission and he hopefully will eliminate with his rifle and scope anyone that wants to bring about the ending of my life on that day. She then said and me, how will I be safe? And not be one to die on that day.

I said because you will be surrounded by bullet proof glass and a brick wall behind you.

You will face towards me away from any building and having glass in front of you and a vest and faith that it will not be your time to leave this earth. She looked at me and said that all of you are the brave ones and that she is a proud coward.

I let her know that your sister will step in front of a bullet to protect you and as I will, so know this; you are in the best hands for your part of this mission. She nodded, and under her breath said I am totally nuts doing this, but I am doing it.

Charlie came to where I was and said that they located Josie and Terri and that they are still by home, for now.

He said that a team from close by is already on their way to them and within an hour should know if the first part of the plan is completed and that the next part will only need a showing off you after a report from a well-protected site, so Lois is safe in having done her part. I agreed and then said, why not have it happen in private in a special site with Lois's face not shown at all only mine. Charlie said good idea but then what, I said she will let everyone know where I will be that day, and hopefully Aziz will be watching.

Charlie just looked at me with that stern face that his uncle would have, when he was about to call me stupid, for what I am suggesting to him right now, he said that after we hear about my family and that they are safe, then we will discuss your suicide. I looked at him and told him no such thing, if I have the team watching my back that day. Charlie just shook his head as he walked away from me.

Everyone had their job to do to get Aziz and I may have the most dangerous one, but I know with these guys with me I should be much safer than going alone.

Now the only thing that mattered in the next day or so is that Josie and Terri were safe and off somewhere that Aziz and his men could not find, and then it was show time and I could not wait to do it, to be able to get Aziz and with his capture, we are almost to Syeed.

And then with any luck it will all be over and peace will finally be had with us.

Now the waiting starts and continues until we get word of any outcome from the teams in St. Louis, and with anticipation of only their safety.

CHAPTER TWENTY-TWO

Just out front of the Star motel at the end of a street of hotels and motels in an area of vacationers and where business people will stay, and make that their base to visit attractions around the city. Josie did pick a good area with thousands of people going in and out of the area without making anyone seem to care or even notice them, for being nothing more than another tourist staying in that area. Heard on the radio was Alpha team in front set, and no sign of objective. Then another radio saying that this is Bravo team out back, the same here.

Charlie listened carefully to every word that they said, and then another voice came on with, this is the spy in the sky, and all seems calm down there. Charlie was doing a Rick with his weapon, rotating it in his hands and sternly looking at the radio like he could see what was going on now. Then like magic, the communications officer brought in a monitor to see what was happening at the site in real time.

This information was being sent from the drone that was up above. Charlie now was feeling better but not much, for he wished he was with the teams.

The only problem with him being there would result in Aziz's death not his capture. And Charlie knew it also, that is what would happen to him.

This is Bravo team, movement coming out back, and this is Alpha team movement out front. Charlie moved closer to the monitor to see what was going on better, and he saw a group coming out the back and with them he saw Terri. In the front the movement was another group this time with his mother Josie. Charlie now knew that they were playing him and that one of them will get away and the other will stay with the captures. So at least one would make Charlie to decide on his next move.

Charlie's mind was racing with any idea that he could to save both. He knew that his mother was a very strong woman and that she would be able to handle the situation, after all she is a James.

So, Charlie radioed the Bravo team to give them some information on Terri, to use in the help in her extraction right now. There was five men walking her to what was probably a vehicle to get away, and Charlie knew that he had one chance to help her be safe.

Again, Charlie was drawn between trying to save his mother or his sister, he hoped both but knew the instant that any gunfire started then the team with them would use their body for protection.

To have this happen with both getting free was something that would be almost impossible to be done, without a distraction from either the front or back.

So, Charlie went with Terri getting free and trying to do the same for his mother, he knew that his mother would be very upset if he freed her and not Terri. So, Charlie thought of what to say to her to let her know he was around to help her.

Jenny came up to Charlie and told him to react as if it was just another mission, and to think what will work on this one. Charlie just smiled and grabbed the radio and spoke into it with the words of Terri do the limbo. Everyone around him looked as if he has just lost it completely, and I knew what he meant. When they were younger, Terri loved to do the limbo at parties that they were at. She would go back and almost touch the ground with her back. Terri would always win the contest, so Charlie radioed and told the team to yell out very loud to Terri. One soldier yelled out, Terri! Charlie says do the limbo! Terri smiled and knew exactly what Charlie meant and she leaned back and with that motion, the Bravo team unleashed a volley of rounds that no man would live through.

Two team members ran up to Terri and grabbed her and took her away.

Charlie's heart pumped with excitement at what he just saw and then it dropped when he saw what he knew would happen after the gunfire.

The ones up front grouped closer together, two men one on either side and one directly behind her.

Two also broke off and hid behind some cars for cover and the three with my mother went calmly to a vehicle.

With Terri being safe now, everyone had their attention locked on his mother, and what was going to happen to her.

Jenny tried to put her arm around Charlie and he then threw it off him and gave her a stare. I walked up to him and smacked him on the back of the head and told him to get his mind on business and not to worry who it was that was just taken, and that we all have an interest in this mission, including Jenny. She looked as if I just said a bad thing and Charlie turned to her and gave her a hug and said thanks. She then turned to me and said thanks with her eyes.

Within minutes Terri was rescued and Josie was taken away to who knows where, and in my mind, I knew more now that I must do what is asked of me. Charlie had a plan before and I had an idea, now we must realize that it just may be a swap that is if Aziz even cares more of me then Josie. With me it is over and with Josie it is me and Charlie, then Terri and after all others who have brought death to Syeed's family and followers, my family, and the team.

I tried to figure out what would satisfy these fanatics since the one they want they already got, but they did not get to consider his eyes, which was something that they would have wanted.

I left Charlie and Jenny to their planning and I decided to take a walk and try and put my own plan together of what they wanted more now than they could have.

I knew that if I did do the television broadcast of my part in the battles years ago, and that I let drop where I would be that day, would they want a swap or try and kill me, or would they want both, or neither.

I thought of all that I have done when Rick and I traveled together and things not about war, but what my life has been up till now and what it should be in the future. It was time to get my head back into the same thoughts that Rick would have in this situation.

It is time to talk to the team without Charlie so we can come up with what might work and how to protect Josie primarily. I wanted to know if Jimmy will be there, and if the black op group will not be far behind. It is time to prepare for the worst tonight.

CHAPTER TWENTY-THREE

The next morning Charlie was sitting at a desk with Jenny and neither was talking, and the team and I came up and asked him what the problem was now. Charlie said, "that he is not sure now why Aziz took his family and what he wants from the abduction of his mother. He also said would the interview do anything to help this situation today."

I sat down and proceeded to inform Charlie that every single one of us including the black op team will do what is necessary to bring your mother back to your side. Charlie just shook his head and that is when Jenny stood up and said "thank you all, and yes we do need each one of you to help us retrieve his mother and to capture Aziz and hopefully find Syeed. But we will start with his mother and work our way to the end of this mission."

Charlie stood up and said "team I have a plan and with this plan there will be danger, but I know that you all will do your best to protect my Uncle Bob from harm. Because he is not only going into the den of the lion, but that he is going to offer a swap for my mother."

Everyone looked a bit shocked at what he just said, but I knew what he already meant of what I was to do, and I was ready in my mind for the next step of this new journey in my life.

Jenny spoke up and said, "that you cannot expect Bob to defend himself after they take him in exchange for your mother, and what makes you think that they would want him instead."

Charlie started to stand up to talk, but I quickly motioned for him to sit down. I stood in the middle of an unbelievable group of people, ones who would give their lives to do the same thing that I am about to do.

I told all of them that I have a plan and I know Charlie will accept it and all I need is all your help. Now, remember if things go bad, the only thing that matters is the safety of Charlie's mom and not me. If needed I will dance my way out of trouble! Smiles, but no laughter!

So, the plan is set and Charlie started to explain it to the team, and that is when I knew they all were tense about it. I entered the room with the sound of some music from the 80's with a disco song about staying alive and came in with what I called a dance, but others well, they would just call it humorous.

And Jenny stood up and danced with me, because she sensed my humor was covering my fear.

And she was right about that, and after the entrance and dance I let everyone know that what is about to begin soon is needed and that I trust every one of you, and do not ever doubt your skills.

Charlie's plan was simple, something just like we have discussed before. He began with telling Lois what he wanted to be said in the interview and to make sure that she does not turn her head towards the camera at any time, so that there will be no chance of discovering her identity, until this is all over. He then said that Lois you will let out like just in the conversation of the next place that Bob will be at. After the interview, Lois, you exit and Bob you act as if you have no idea that the camera is still running, and start with your statement of the people that you have killed to get to St Louis to save Rick's sister.

After we leave the team will already be mostly in position and the rest will be ready by the time you arrive at the cemetery to visit Rick's grave site. We have every possible area covered and if by chance they have a sniper, Jimmy and his spotter will locate him. Jake and Riley will be close by as well as Jenny. I will be walking with you. I stopped him with that part of his plan and said that you will be in a very safe place and let the others cover me. If you become emotional after they bring your mother out, if they bring her out. That will not help our mission in any way at all. He agreed and then continued with the plan.

Charlie said that we are leaving the spot where they took the shot at you and my mother clear; because we hope that they will feel comfortable going back there and setting up the shooter again. So, we will have every place covered all around you and the drone will be watching movement around that we cannot see from the ground.

And now we should have some type of call word that you will say in case you feel the whole thing is going sideways on us. I told them that I will use the phrase Chuck misses you! And get her and me to the ground.

If by chance that they have her too far away from me and making it hard to get a clean shot and a get away without either one of us getting hurt, then I must improvise the situation and you will also. I told Jimmy that Rick and I had a signal when we were in trouble, or when I was. I would tap right or left leg and that was the direction I would move to for him to take the shot. I also tapped my butt then I dropped on it so he could get the shot better. Jimmy looked at me and said you two were coordinated all right. He then told me that he will do his best and I told him that is all I can expect from him.

Charlie came by me and said that if my uncle was here, he wouldn't let you do this would he. I smiled at Charlie and said Rick would have told me when you get in the middle of it, turn and smile because I am right with you looking through my scope. And that is the trust I have of you and your entire team.

Charlie and Jenny went back to going over the plan that they have put together, and each time it turns out differently than before, someone always dies and Charlie said that what are we missing in this plan that won't have someone die. Jenny looked at him and said only luck.

CHAPTER TWENTY-FOUR

Decision time! 6:00 A.M. and everyone was up and fully prepared to go, except me. I got up groggy and wanting my coffee, and a little to eat. I walked into the mess area and asked the guy that was doing the cooking today, in what I thought would be a funny way, and can I have my last meal now. As I said that, to me it was to break up the tension, but to these brave people that were about to enter battle probably today, not funny at all. Charlie and Jenny came up to me and said, Bob relax, we have it all figured out now. I looked at them and told them that I am glad you do, because I feel that my belly wants to burst right now. Jenny gave me a hug and said we will not let anything happen to you, got it.

I nodded and smiled a smile that was truly a phony one and I feel that they knew that it was also.

I knew that they had no new plan and that in each scenario I die. Oh, well had a good run as they say in the movies.

Lois sat by me and asked me how I could do this well knowing that you may be killed today.

I told her that my family is safe and my daughter will have people looking after her and that Rick gave his all for me and his family and I could only do the same for him today. Mind you I have no death wish, but if it is meant to be, then so be it.

I finished my breakfast and had my coffee, then went to the bathroom and finished getting dressed. I went to Jimmy first and gave him a quick hug and as I did tell him not to miss today, he smiled and said he would not miss today. I went next to Riley and Jake and did the same but told them, no matter what get Charlie's mother out before me; they both just nodded and patted my back as I left them. I then went to the rest of the team and thanked them all for their service not only to the country, but the service of today with me. Then I gave a little tap dance and said that is my signal that I am running. They all laughed and said we know you will not run, unless his mom is with you. I nodded and said than let's get this over, before I change my mind. Charlie then said Bob I know that you would never change your mind, so yes, let's go!

Lois and I went to a building that was just outside of our camp, and we entered and were surprised at all the technical television items that were already set up. She looked at her sister and said you guys our as good if not better than my station.

I looked around and saw where she would be sitting and the spot that I would also, and mine looked as if I was to be interrogated, with a single chair in the middle of a room with lights all around me. Lois saw my face and said that we need all the lights, but the chair, that must go.

I agreed and so did Charlie, he had a nice chair brought in, something that you would see in a waiting area of some type of office.

I sat in the chair, but could not get used to all the lights that were directed at me. Jenny said that by all the lights on you Bob, Lois will be just a shadow. I told her I understand now and I just hope I do not melt from all the heat they are giving off. Lois laughed and said try these lights with a pound of makeup on! I smiled and said no thank you, and we were almost ready to do a quick run through before we tape the show.

And then after it was over I would leave and they would broadcast it as if it was live. And everyone else would get set up at the position we had picked out and wait.

The run through was mostly Lois saying Bob calm down, just think of the camera as Aziz and talk to him, but not to directly. Ok, so I am camera shy and the thought of so many people that were about to watch me talk on this station does give me some willies.

So, I focused on the camera as if it was Rick standing there and I became so much calmer and we started to tape the real one now.

I was already sweating and the lights just came on, but that was fear not heat. Lois started with Bob you have been through a lot six years ago, how did it all start.

I began with on that July 4th day in my apartment complex listening to the birds at early morning and watching people begin their day with packing up the cars or cleaning the grill for the afternoon cooking, and then hearing the news that terrorist was attacking our country, and that it was going on all over the country at the same time.

A man name Rick James, a former special operations sniper, pulled us all together to fight those who have disgraced our soil. Lois was quick with, disgraced our soil, those are harsh words Bob aren't they. I looked directly into the camera and said that those people were savages and did not deserve to bleed on our great soil in America. They were cowards and not a regular army, but a group of people that think what they did would ever stop us from having the life and liberty that we have had since the beginning of our country.

Ridding our country of that scum was the thing we all did best those years ago. They had us at first until we brought ourselves together and fought them back to the desert that they came from.

I was getting so wound up talking about what happened years ago, and how I wished that my friend Rick was here now to help us take this fight to them again. I took a breath and Lois mentioned of all the men and woman that were killed by the insurgents and how many that your friend Rick and you killed on your travels around the country. I smiled as I told her that each one of those scum bags deserved to die and I know that they are not getting any virgins in heaven, because that is not where they have ended up at.

She smiled at that statement and said but Bob, are they not back trying to do the same thing now. I told her that they are here to get even from all the deaths that I have had a part in and the death of one of the brothers that Rick shot in the head in Afghanistan years before that day here. I smirked and said that he shot this guy from a trash dump as his shooting spot. Funny isn't it that he shot that trash from a trash site.

Charlie and some of the team did what they could from not cheering as I talked of what Rick and I did. Charlie wrote on a piece of paper, give them hell Bob. Make them want to run without worry to your site and let this team finish yours and Ricks work.

I took out a rag I had in my pocket and wiped my forehead and looked back at the camera. Lois and I talked for some time and I kept going after the people that I wanted to go after.

I wanted them to want to see me kneel and have a fantasy of beheading me. I did say fantasy, did I not? And that is what I tried to do during that interview.

As we were wrapping up the show I knew that I needed something to say to get them to make a trade. I told Lois as she thanked me and started to get up to leave. I again looked deep into that camera and said, to the men that have taken a mother and tried to take her daughter as hostages, for what I cannot imagine. Why do you think that harming innocent woman will make you all so powerful in the eyes of Allah?

What that does is shows how much of a coward you all are and that even Allah laughs at what you have done. So, I offer myself in exchange for the women. Yes, a man for woman that should get your interest up. I will give a place later that I will be at, so you and I can make an exchange of the one woman for me. I am the partner of the man that killed your brother and so many of your followers.

Lois already gave the site that I would be at that day and I just said that for them to feel that I will not have set a trap there but will at the place I said I will tell them later.

Now things were getting in motion now, and we will see if they take the bait of where I will be at first. Charlie came up to me and said, "Uncle Bob I didn't think that you would actually offer yourself up in exchange for my mother." I told him that if at the time, he will exchange us, I will do it to get your mother free from them.

Lois came up and said, 'wow Bob! They must be twirling in their skirts right now. And Jenny said after that, Bob do you really know what you just offered." I said yes Jenny; I have offered my freedom for Charlie's mother's freedom. She gave me a hug and then said "that the team will do whatever is necessary to ensure your safety today and that we are all proud now." I looked at the team and said that remember the mission is Josie, Charlie's mother, and that I am second, got it.

They all nodded at me and Jimmy said I will take the mole off the face of any person that tries to harm you. I said thanks, but how about just kill him. He smiled and gave thumbs up.

CHAPTER TWENTY-FIVE

Lois left for her station and I started to leave also, but I was going to a fate that I had no idea of what it would be. I know that the team and Charlie will completely cover me has brought in the special operations team that he had following Aziz's men. So, I should feel better, but I have that feeling that Rick would get when he felt some type of trouble coming our way. I continued my way out and stopped for a second and took a quick look around at everyone and saw nothing but complete professionalism, as they went about their duties to get ready to leave also. They should arrive about a half hour ahead of me and be setting up in plenty of time of my arrival.

I got into a car that they had for me, they felt a car looked more like I would be alone. A truck or SUV would give an impression that some others were riding along with me because of the size. In the car was to be one man in the trunk and one in the back seat that they took out to give him more room. The guy in the trunk had a radio set up and a quick release to open the trunk for him to get out of it as fast as he needed to.

They both were very well equipped and know their business, because of the training that they have had and the direction that Charlie has given to each of them so to not make this mission a failure, and that I will and Josie will make it back to our families safe.

We are going to the cemetery and should be close to Rick's grave site and I will be waiting for my new friends to arrive, if they watched the show and noticed when Lois mentioned that I will be here in the afternoon.

There is a lot of if's that are happening now and I only hope that they do show up and have Josie with them for a trade. And I know that if they show and the team is ready, we both could leave there safe. If for some reason things change then we should do a Rick and wing it.

As I was driving to my destination my radio com in my ear was crackling and then Charlie said to me, "have faith in us today and do not be a hero to try and save my mother."

I arrived at the cemetery and pulled into a regular parking spot and proceeded to get out of the car and I heard the trunk pop and a squeak and a dam it from the back seat. You see in the back was Riley and the trunk Jake, both are built like a house and did what they could to squeeze into their hiding spots in the car.

As I exited the car I looked around in a manner of admiring the landscape and then walked to my designated spot that I would stand and hopefully be covered with the team. I heard another crackle on my ear com and this time it was Jimmy.

"Bob, just remember what you told me about yours and Rick's signal, and tap your side to move to." Then silence again, for it was so close to show time.

I was approximately a hundred yards from the headstone and with each step, I felt someone watching me. But not the men and women assigned to me but others! I had that feeling! And right now, it was not a good one.

I looked over by the mausoleums and saw a glimmer of light coming from a tree beside it; I thought that it couldn't be Jimmy for he would never be so careless to have any shinning objects on himself during a mission. So, I now know why I am having that feeling right now, and that is because someone else is there and I bet that he or she is not a friend of mind.

I was now ten yards away from the site and I heard Charlie say to me to have faith in us, and then I heard Jenny say "Bob I need you to move just a little to your right so we can have a clean shot at anyone that may show up at the site now." I was just about to move to my right when I heard a rifle shot and it almost hit me if I was not slow to move. Jenny shirked and told Riley and Jake to move and acquire the asset, this mission is over!

They were about ten or fifteen yards away from me when I heard another shot and then Riley was down, Jake moved to him and another shot and he was down also. And another shot but this time it came from Jimmy and you saw a figure drop from that tree and Jimmy say aloud, "that is for you two guys."

I dropped to my knees and waited for my faith, now that my bodyguards were gone. I looked around and this time I saw a man coming out of the woods and only knew that it was not someone that I would want too.

On my ear com, I heard a crackle and Charlie saying to me to "stay and wait for we have this," then Jenny saying "Bob stay down and do not move." Then another crackle and this voice said that no matter what we do, you will die today. Jenny broke in and said, "that they have our radios now, and that we have to break off communications now." Jimmy broke in and said to me, "Bob remember the last move you did and I will be with you." Then silence again!

I did remember it but was not sure that the new members of our team also knew it. Jenny came back on and said that they just came on and anything before was only ours.

I got up and stood facing the man that was approaching me after just coming out of the woods. He had his hands up and walked towards me slowly and did not even make any motion by turning his head around in search of anyone watching him.

He knew that we must have some others besides the two that were just shot and that did not seem to concern him at all, he has a role to play now and that is to draw all eyes to him and have an opening where others were to exit from different areas around us. Charlie tried immediately to figure out how they knew of our plan today.

Jenny told him that they must have some type of listening device near our camp, and one other member of the team mentioned of all the equipment that they took off the ones that were either killed or captured lately, we have it in a closet in camp and they must have the device in that stuff.

Charlie said again we underestimated our enemy of having the knowledge of warfare just as we do.

The man stopped a few feet from me and he continued to keep his hands up and said nothing at all to me. Then suddenly the cemetery looked like a war zone with our people and theirs all coming out and not one gunshot yet. Charlie and Jenny stayed back and out of sight not for protection, but for their observation of what is happening here.

They needed to observe to make our next move without wondering when bullets will fly.

A small group of men all together came out and in the middle of them was Aziz and Charlie's mother Josie. They made a wall around them so no one could get a safe shot at him without accidently hitting Josie.

As the circle of men came closer to me, I could see Josie now. On her face was not a look of fear but that of anger, along with a look of determination to get away at whatever cost to her without any more casualties to any of our team.

I also saw sadness as she looked straight into my eyes that can only be of what she feels that she has put us all through, that would be in her mind not ours. We all know that only one person causes this whole situation, and that is Syeed, not Josie.

The circle opened a little, enough for Aziz and Josie to be seen by me and hard for any other to. Aziz spoke with a thick Middle Eastern accent and said to me; "Bob you called me a coward for taking this woman, did you not." I nodded yes and added that are you not one by that action. He smiled and said that "a coward takes a woman for no reason, but I did what I did to achieve today." I looked at him and asked him what he meant by that statement and he answered with; "you are in front of me now, are you not?"

Charlie and Jenny now was beginning to become extremely worried at what was next in this mad man's mind right now. He seems to be so confident at his presence here with all our people so close to him. Charlie said to Jenny that he feels that this man has a plan to escape us today and only wondered if he would take someone with him or just attempt to kill some of us as he leaves here.

Charlie kept hitting his head with his hand in anger of what he feels is his stupidity of trying to second guess this man as if he was just a simple person just following orders without any knowledge of warfare at all. Today he knows that he was wrong and his adversary was the one in front of us in this cat and mouse game that we have found ourselves in today.

Jenny told Charlie that we have many choices and he has a few, he should trade and hopefully get away, to fight and die today. We have fight and sacrifice those two for the mission, to trade and hopefully we have a chance to rescue those that he will take with him, or we can rely on Jimmy's rifle to at least get Aziz and Bob has a knife strapped to the back of his neck and he attacks those left with him trying to get Josie away without harm.

But the last option, only me and Jimmy knew, it was a combination of the others and one that we hope will at least save Josie today. So, all of us just waited for the other to make the first move, I decided not to wait and I brought my hands up to the back of my neck as if I was in a surrendering pose. Josie now had fear in her eyes and slowly shook her head side to side in a no gesture. At the same time, I went to my neck two of his men brought their weapons up to my chest, and with that I slowly put my hands back down to my side.

Now I know that I am in the presence of soldiers, not just some ordinary men with guns. I quickly decided on plan B, now my trust was in Jimmy and his shooting ability.

I had to get just a little closer to Josie if any plan I have working in my head will have any chance of working without a dreadful ending.

I took two steps forward as I said to Aziz on his intentions that he has on this situation of Josie and I, and I took one more step forward for my balance to be better, then Aziz said that you will not get any closer to me if you want to live. I then smiled and said you can't blame a guy for trying can you.

He smiled and said, 'it will be an honor to kill such a formidable enemy as yourself, and I only wished that I could have considered your friends Rick's eyes as he died that day." Josie squirmed at that statement, but Aziz made no acknowledgement of her movement, he was on me.

Aziz said, 'that we will trade, and you will go back to Syeed and he will have the honor as the elder, to have your head fed to the animals." I looked at him and said you have it all figured out except that what happens when we trade and Josie is far away from us, and a flurry of gunfire heads our way, having me be collateral damage. He said that after the trade you will see the rest of my plan.

Charlie and Jenny listen into the conversation and now tried to figure out what he could do after some type of trade with me.

They went over many ways for him at least to get out after he either killed the two of us or grabbed us and ran through the hail of bullets that would be shot at all of us to get him.

After giving Charlie a little time for his plan to get back together and for me getting all the courage that I could get, to take my last step and to have mine and Jimmy's plan to go into effect now.

With no going, back, I put my hand down and patted my right side of my butt. I moved to Josie and grabbed her hands as if I was saying goodbye, then I put a strong grip on her, her eyes opened when I did that knowing that something was about to happen.

I told her to stay loose for this all will be over soon, right Aziz I said. She went along with what I had planned with loosening up her body for me to do my thing, which I truly hope will work.

I dropped backwards and down on my butt at the same time I pulled Josie down on top of me. At the instant that I started to fall back, I heard a rifle fire and I looked at Aziz, and he was hit directly in the chest and he fell back also. I rolled Josie off me and reached back and took out the knife I had strapped to the back of my neck and shoulders. I took a swipe at the two that were on my right in hopes that someone will get the two on my left.

I got both on the upper thigh and started to get up to defend myself, because I knew that what I just did to the two would not keep either down very long. Before I was up I heard another shot and one of the men were down and I signaled to get Josie.

But before anyone could even get close to us, one on my left hit me over the head with his rifle and the last thing I heard was a vehicle coming fast to us. In that vehicle were Aziz's men. They stopped and took his body and put it into the vehicle, at that moment I thought that it was over for now, but I was so wrong.

CHAPTER TWENTY-SIX

When I woke up, Josie was close to me but we were not with Charlie and his team, we were with Aziz's men, and they were not very happy with me right now. I slowly got up in a sitting position and when I did one of the men slapped me and spoke in a language I did not understand. Another came up and said for me to thank Allah that I am not dead now, because we have orders to bring you in.

I asked the one that spoke English what he meant with bring me in. He said that the almighty Syeed will have his revenge on you for his brothers. I then asked him why he brought the woman, and he said that Syeed wants his revenge of his killer's family for his family. I now knew that I needed to get information to Charlie. They took my ear radio bud out and stepped on it, but what they didn't know was that I also had a radio transmitter put into my belt buckle so when needed I could activate it, I felt that if things went bad, as they have, that I can get information to Charlie and his team. It would not be detected by any type of equipment that locate radio waves, since I will turn it on after they do their scan.

Back at the cemetery, Charlie and his team could not believe what just happened. Charlie said that Bob and Jimmy put a plan B together and it worked. The one problem was that we did not react quick enough to save my mother and Bob. Bob risked his life to free my mother and Jimmy took out Aziz, which was a great thing, but we all froze at what happened and did not do our duty today. Jenny then spoke and said that we were not expecting these people to have any type of military expertise, and they did.

Charlie said now we should make our plans that involve a military type of combatant. The team then brought the bodies of Riley and Jake to transport them to the airport to go back home for the last time. Charlie of all people was saddened by what happened to them, for they were his two best friends not only that they were his bodyguards too. And after all of this he will never accept another bodyguard, for he feels that he should be able to guard himself.

Josie asked me if I was all right and one the men told her to shut up and only speak when spoken to. I now know that we are not going to be able to communicate to escape. I asked a very simple question and that was if we both could have some water to drink. A man stood up and said that Aziz cannot have a drink of water now, so why should you two have it. I said because we are all human beings and that what happens in war should not make anyone suffer needlessly for it. He laughed at my words and walked away from us.

I looked at Josie and said that I am sorry for not completing the mission. She smiled and when they were not looking asked me "if I had another plan?"

I let her know that now it is up to your son. She then said "how will Charlie know of where we are at?" I looked back and pushed down on my buckle, that had a B on it and with a finger I slid it like a toggle switch, and smiled at her and said that is how he knows.

Charlie was feeling sorry for himself because he did not save his mother let alone Bob, but when he was talking to Jenny a radio came on and it sounded just like Bob. Charlie looked at Jimmy and said what did you two come up with, and how do we communicate with him. Jimmy said that he will let you know where they are at and you will be able to only hear. Charlie slammed his hand down on the table and said that he needs more. Jenny calmly went to him and slapped him and told him that Bob will give us all the information that we need for now.

Jimmy came up to Charlie and said that he wanted to go to Bob's daughter and tell her of what has happened today. Jenny agreed, but Charlie said that she should not know of this until we have better news of him. Jimmy disagreed and so did the rest of the team. Jenny said that Samantha has been through a lot before and she knows that she will be able to understand what Jimmy says to her, and that he is the one to do it. Charlie agreed and Jimmy was off.

Josie asked me what I feel will happen to us, and I said that I do not want to think of what will happen to you, but that I will be beheaded for my sins against Syeed.

She asked me what can she do now, and I said to be strong, that your son is not far away. And with that statement, Charlie heard it and agreed with the fact that he will get to us soon. He then said aloud, Bob just keep talking because we are listening right now.

CHAPTER TWENTY-SEVEN

$7:30$ p.m.... on time for a commercial flight, much more comfortable than the military transports that I usually take Jimmy said to himself. Jimmy landed in New Jersey and walked down the walk way and entered the terminal and to his surprise, standing waiting for his exit from the plane was the smiling face of Samantha.

She went to him and said that Jenny said that you have some time off and decided to come here to visit me, wow I am honored. Jimmy stumbled as he walks because he knew why he was here today, yes to see her but to inform Samantha of her father's imprisonment.

Samantha tried desperately to help Jimmy, but he would have none of her helping. Not that he didn't think she could help him but that he was a true gentleman let her know that he can and will carry his own. Jimmy laughed at Samantha as she nonstop talked to him about everything. He turned to her and with a smile said do you ever run out of things to say, and she smiled and said that she always talks too much when she is nervous.

Jimmy said to her that there is nothing to be nervous about, I came to visit and that should not make you feel uneasy now right. She looked at him and said, Jimmy either you like me or something bad has happened to my dad. Jimmy stopped and looked at her and said that he is here for both reasons but my feelings must wait.

Samantha put her arm through his and they made their way to her vehicle. After they got in and Samantha said that she has an extra room and that she already has it ready for him, then she went silent all the way to her place. When they arrived, Jimmy started to get out and Samantha started to cry, and Jimmy being the by the book military guy, had no idea what to do. So, he did what his mother would do when he started to cry and that was to put her arm around him and tell him that everything will be better soon. Samantha cried even harder now, and Jimmy was lost.

After they entered her place and Jimmy put his things into the room that she had ready for him, they sat down on the couch together. She looked at him with eyes that could make you melt and with sadness of what she feels is coming. Jimmy started with, "you dad is a hero!" She heard that and broke down and cried so hard that he didn't even want to touch her. She looked at him and said "he is dead, isn't he?" Jimmy scrambled with his words now and said "no he is not dead! But he has been captured by Aziz's men and we are trying to locate him." She sank down into his chest and said what happened.

He told her of the plan and how it went bad. He said that your father gave a signal for me to shoot and when I did I killed Aziz and a few of his men, he pulled Charlie's mom on him to protect her and pulled out his knife and slashed two of his men. But another hit him and a vehicle appeared and took both your dad and Charlie's mom.

Jenny said that we have a way to follow them for now and we will. I promise you that I will get to him wherever he is at and make sure he is safe. Samantha looked at him and said, Jimmy please do not promise me, but only do your best. He looked at her, and she said that is what Rick would do.

Samantha asked Jimmy how it went and why did he do it. He said that most of the plan was your dad's and he wanted to be sure that he was close to Josie to do what was necessary to get her free. But we all underestimated our enemy and they were much better prepared than we gave them credit for. They had a plan against our plan because they had a radio in our camp that they left with a man that we captured, and he was a plant.

Jimmy then said, "that they knew everything that we were about to do, and that when we arrived at what we thought was our trap, it was theirs. They killed both Riley and Jake, you remember them, big as a house guys. Your dad tried to run to help them but that is when it all went bad. For an old guy, he sure has guts and some motioned in his step."

Samantha smiled and said 'that I know that my dad will be ok and that he will get Charlie's mom out safe, because that is what my dad does." Jimmy looked at Samantha and told her that "we all need that type of mindset to get through all of this."

CHAPTER TWENTY-EIGHT

Charlie was sitting at his table with it completely covered with papers and maps, constantly going through them he was trying to figure out where we were at and what was the next move that his enemy has planned. With his fingers running through his hair and pulling on it every so often, blaming himself for how this all happened and that he missed the outcome of what he felt was an easy mission.

While Charlie is emerged in his disappointment of his past misfortune of the mission that went so wrong, his commanding officer entered the room. Charlie was so out of it at the time that he didn't even stand and salute as he should have. The commander looked at him and said that is it that bad that you forget protocol and not salute me. Charlie then stood and as he was just about to give his commander a salute, the commander came to him and gave him a compassionate slap on the shoulder instead. He said, "that this stuff happens to the best of us, in fact, your uncle had some missions that went completely wrong and people got hurt because if it, but he bounced back and made it better by learning from his mistakes."

Charlie told the commander that he understands what he is saying and that he is so proud to have the same commander as his uncle. Charlie said, "that he sometimes feels that his uncle had put the two of us together so you can sort of take care of me, and feel that his uncle is watching him also." The commander said, "that when your uncle left us, I felt obligated to be your commander; your uncle would have wanted that also. And Charlie your feeling is right, Rick will always be looking over you, but he has so much faith in your competence and training." Charlie gave a weird look at the commander at that statement and said, "looking over me?" The commander said yes, "wherever he is now, hopefully in a very nice place." Charlie gave a head motion of that he understood, and then the two sat down and the commander asked him what he could do to help him in his dilemma, that he feels will get corrected.

Jenny walked into the room and right after her, Jimmy was back from New Jersey and he came in and they all sat down and the new mission planning started. Jenny first asked Jimmy how Samantha took the news of her father. He said that she is a strong woman and understood the situation and felt that all will be ok. The commander looked at Jimmy and asked him who Samantha was, and he told him that she is Bob's daughter and that he went in person to tell her. The commander smiled and said if she is anything like her old man she understands.

Charlie then informed the commander that Jenny had a small transmitter installed in Bob's belt buckle and he turned it on.

The commander looked startled at the fact that Jenny and Bob thought ahead like that, and wanted to know whose idea was it. Jenny said that Bob wanted a little insurance just in case, and I had the communication officer to rig one up.

The commander said, "with what you know now any idea of the area at least they might be hiding the two of them."

Charlie tried to say this gently to the commander, but we have no idea where they are now. He asked Jenny, "that if you took someone around here where would you feel would be a safe place to hide for a short period until arrangements were made to transport them to the location that they really want them to go to."

Jenny said to him, "that is exactly what I have been racking my brain about, on where would I go and I still can't figure it out." Then Charlie spoke up and said, "that they are from the Middle East and that should make a difference in what area that they would go to and hide until the right time to move them." Jimmy said, "that if I took someone and was hiding them and did not want anyone to know that I had hostages, maybe some type of warehouse or abandoned building of some type."

The commander said now we are cooking and let's keep going with these ideas. Charlie and Jenny now finally felt that they may be getting somewhere and smiled at each other and went back to the maps on the table. Jimmy began to look at different buildings that would give a sniper a good advantage to shoot at any intruders. The commander sat back and said that I feel my duty is about done for now.

CHAPTER TWENTY-NINE

Josie looked over at me and said, "Bob do you really feel that we will get out of this, and not be killed." I smiled and said "that Charlie your son is doing the impossible and he will not give up until we are safe." She smiled and said, "thanks for the hope at least." At that exact moment, the communications officer barged into the room with the others and said that he has sound again, it left him for a period until he adjusted the frequency.

They all gathered around the radio and even the commander did not move or make a sound now. On the radio, they heard Bob saying to Josie how her son will not give up looking for us even if we were unable to be found in a building with impenetrable walls and low ceilings with a stinky sulfur smell all around us. Jenny sprang up from her chair and said Bob just gave us our first clue.

They all started to think of what I meant with my clues, and Jimmy spoke first with, walls, ceilings, and sulfur, I say sewers. Charlie and Jenny at almost the exact same time said bingo, you may be right.

For a second we had a quick laugh at what just happened. The commander said now we should guess where in the sewers they are.

The communications officer said that the reception is still very good so they must be close to the surface or by some type of opening to get out.

As Charlie was bringing out the maps of the city roads, that would also give a little idea of the sewers in the city. Another crackle on the radio and this time Bob began to say that he has never been to the beach around here and Josie said when and if we get out of here that not far away is that water park that enters the park, you know the one that Rick did not make it out of. Not far from that water tower where Rick shot that guy and he feels about 500 feet from it.

Charlie's brain went into overdrive and said beach scratch that because there is none here, water park the only water into the park was the stream, and the tower that Uncle Rick shot that man, 500 feet, well it is only 50 feet to the ground, so 500 feet away from the tower with thick walls and low ceilings and the smell of sulfur as a sewer would have. Let's get going to the park for a much closer look.

Charlie assembled the entire team, including the special operations team, and stood as he talked and let them know that we may have a location of my mother and Bob.

They all looked at him for his next order, and Jimmy stood up instead and told all of them that we are not in any practice run and that the two that are being held hostage will be freed today.

Not far away from them, others have a completely different plan then Charlie and that theirs is just about to begin and after that, it will be harder if not impossible to find the two hostages and free them.

One man entered the room and spoke in broken English that we are about to be moved and when we arrive at our destination, we are to be taken to Syeed for him to decide on your deaths. Josie now started to get nervous and I told her that her son would not let anything ever to happen to her and that I may be dog meat, but you will feel the free air of freedom from your spot on the rocks.

Now Charlie and Jenny were trying to interpret my words and they were having a very hard time of it. At the same time, Josie started to tell me of that one day that her family and she went to the park not far from the duck pond and would throw bread into the stream, and we tried not to have it go by the sewer inlet and that after that we were going to start our day by the water tower and proceed to the road by the freeway.

Charlie then remembered that area and he said that we are about to go and save my mother and Bob. The whole team said that whatever it took that they are in.

Just when Josie finished her story, half dozen men walked into the room and we were escorted out of it into a vehicle that was waiting for us.

CHAPTER THIRTY

As we left where we were kept at, I noticed that two Vehicles were parked outside. One was a white limo with an S symbol on the rear fender and the other was a red sedan. As we were escorted to where they were parked Josie was taken to the limo and I the sedan. I quickly said to the men that were on either side of me why the woman gets the white limo with that big S on the rear fender and you are going to drive me in the red sedan. Seems a little unfair that I don't get the same type of car, and I also guess that she is the first car and mine the second one. The one man said does it matter the car since you both will die the same. I said at least I will still be able to face my executioner, because that is something that I truly want to do.

I only hope that Charlie pickup on the cars and know that Josie is first and that I want to stay with these men to hopefully get to Syeed.

And we were in and on our way to who knows where right now, and with an army of men and woman following us to rescue Josie and track me.

We have been driving on the same four lane road for about 20 minutes and none of my escorts were very interested in my conversation at all. I kept trying to get idea of where we were headed and no such luck on that info from these guys.

I was wondering how Josie was doing in her car and if she is being abused at all. I knew that she is a very strong woman and would rather die before letting those men abuse her in any way. So, I kept trying to get anything that I could from my men, and always came back to Syeed and where does he want to kill me at. And again, no information about that but they did say, that what you would like for your last meal, we know you Americans give your death row people a last meal. I said with a smile, what do you recommend that I should have for my last meal when we get to my, destination?

One said that where you are ending up at, goat is the main meal, and sand if you do not keep your mouth closed when the wind blows. They all laughed and I now know that I will eventually end up in the Middle East somewhere soon, unless Charlie and the team get me out of here first. And I always wanted to go to the Middle East where Rick hunted his pray for the military.

I again hoped that Charlie understood that if they take me to Syeed, I will be able to give them my basic location and a team of crazy military types will be rushing into where I am at and finally end this whole nightmare and kill Syeed.

We continued for a few more minutes and got off the road at an exit and came to a cross road, Josie went left and we turned right, then I spoke up and said that if we are going to the same place why is she going left on Wilson road and I am going right. The one man which I feel is the leader of this group said that it does not matter for you both will be together soon in the place that we are going to.

I knew that if Charlie is to save his mother that now was the best time, when not all the men were in the same spot and that if something went on and they did have the opportunity to rescue Josie, then they would rush me to where I am to go to. And I will be happy for Charlie's mother and proud that I will be face to face with Syeed, the man that orchestrated the death of my best friend and terrorized this entire nation for such a long time back then.

We drove for about ten minutes and on their radio, I heard panic, and gunfire. I now know that the team is doing their job saving Josie and I only hope that they kill them all, because I feel that they abused her, that is why the limo. I sat back in the seat and smiled, then said is there anything wrong guys. And can I help in any way, like put a gun to your head and let you die without all the pain that I feel you are about to have. They turned to me and said that Allah will protect us and that you will die a sinner. I again smiled and said that it was ok with me that I sin, because you will die without your virgins tonight.

They looked at me and punched me in the face and I was out. But just as I was going out I hoped that, they got Josie out and eliminated all the men that had her, and I was out.

CHAPTER THIRTY-ONE

On Wilson Rd heading East a battle was going on and the outcome was still undecided. Charlie and Jenny were battling Syeed's men and they were not standing down to their firepower, because as they fired at the vehicle that Charlie was in, three other vehicles from the team pulled up and opened fire on the insurgents, all watching where they shot because of Josie was in that car. The vehicle that she was in stopped completely for those escorting Josie to get out and stand their ground to fight and that is what gave Josie her chance to escape her captures, and she started to run to where Charlie was at, and was now finally feeling that she would be free of her captures, and reunite with her son.

Meanwhile in my car the men heard from Josie's vehicle just before it all broke out and one of the men said to me, how were they able to know where the two of you were at. I looked at the guy and said how I would know what way that they had to find her. He looked at me and said that you are right; they found her not you, so she must have had some type of GPS on her to locate her. And I said and if I had one, you would be attacked by now.

He smiled and said she is smarter than you I guess. I nodded and said I guess so. The whole time knowing that it was me and not her, so now they feel I am clean for now and can continue to broadcast my information over to Charlie. Next stop Syeed, I feel.

The fighting continued by where Charlie and the team was at, and Josie was getting closer to her son and Jenny was yelling at her to run and head in her direction because it was not in the line of fire from either one. Josie stumbled a few times but that was from sure panic and not having her mind on what was happening but only that she was near her son.

As Josie was about twenty yards away the insurgents turned in her direction and started to open fire at her now. Charlie started to panic at the sight of his mother being shot at and was just about to move towards her when, Jenny sprinted up and went to her aide.

Jenny ran like a rabbit going in different directions to stay out of the direct line of fire and to hopefully draw the fire from Josie and have them shoot at her instead. When Josie and Jenny were within touching distance, Jenny saw one man aim at her and she pranced on Josie to cover her from the shot that seemed to be a direct hit if she didn't take Josie down first.

Josie started to move from underneath Jenny to get moving again, but Jenny did not move and when Josie turned back over she saw blood all over her vest.

At the sight of her blood, Josie screamed and that made Charlie look over in their direction. When he saw that his mother was ok but that Jenny was not moving, he called out to Jimmy to cover him as he ran to her.

Charlie started to sprint to where Jenny and his mother were at; his mother would not leave Jenny's side. Just as Charlie made it within five yards of them he heard a familiar sound, and that was Jimmy's rifle finding his target. When he arrived by his mother and Jenny's spot, he noticed that his mother had a large amount of blood on herself, and it was not from Jenny. Josie looked down at her belly and saw the blood and Charlie saw that Jenny had a bad wound on her shoulder area. Now he signaled the others to cover him to help them get away from the shooting. Josie got up on her own, much pain, but she did it. And Jenny needed more help than Charlie alone. Two others seeing what transpired by Jenny and Josie headed to help and Jimmy continued to do his part and bring one at a time down to meet Allah.

With help Josie made it back to cover and with Charlie's help Jenny did also. Within a few more minutes the team destroyed the enemy and was not able to save anyone of them to question. The only hope of where Bob may be heading now was from one man that said Syeed will have the final satisfaction in beheading your friend where his brother had died by his friend Rick. Then he expired, and only the words that he said is what they needed to figure out quickly before Bob is lost forever.

Josie heard the statement from the dying man and she said that she knew where they may be taking Bob and that it will not be easy to locate him and can possible save him. Charlie looked at his mother and asked her where you think that they are taking him, and she said, Afghanistan!

CHAPTER THIRTY-TWO

The team finished cleaning up as Charlie and another rushed Jenny and his mother to the nearest medical center. Josie was shot in the thigh and what Charlie made of it, the bullet stayed in the fatty area and not a major vein. Jenny was a little more serious since she was shot in the shoulder but very close to the heart, the shot just missed her vest, the bullet came in from the side and through her top of the shoulder through to her chest, and was losing a great deal of blood on the way to get taken care of.

One of his team was driving and his mother sat in the front seat, well actually kind of laid sideways on her other side of the gun shot. Charlie was in the back seat with Jenny and she was lying on his legs, as he stroked her hair and tried to comfort her until they got to where they were going. Josie just looked at Charlie and Jenny, with the thought that these two will be together after all this is over, mark my word she said to herself. And then gave a sigh of happiness for them.

They made it to a hospital and drove almost into it by the emergency room entrance.

The soldier that was driving jumped out and ran inside, when inside he basically ordered the staff to hurry and go to the vehicle because two people were shot in a battle just now and they need immediate care. One nurse asked him who you think you are, and almost at the same time the phone rang and another nurse ran up and whispered in her ear and they both took off to the car. The soldier had no idea who was on the phone but he didn't care because they were all coming out and making sure that they were being taken care of, doctors and even a maintenance man with a bucket to clean up our car.

They took Josie out of the car first, and went to the back to get Jenny out. When they moved, her she gave out a loud moan from pain, and Charlie screamed at them and told them to be careful because she is an American war hero. Everyone stopped and proceeded with extreme care after Charlie's outburst.

A doctor already gave her a sedative as they were taking her out and as Jenny started to drift off from it, she looked up at Charlie and said, Charlie you fool, I love you so much and then was off in dreamland. Charlie froze at that statement from her.

He sat back down in the car and tried to regain his military composer after what she said.

The rest of the team showed up and set up a perimeter around the hospital.

The staff started to ask Charlie why the protection and he said that do you remember about six years ago, what happened in this country, and one nurse came up and said yes, I do and now I remember who you are.

You are the nephew of the man that fought that battle in the park to save us. He said yes that was my Uncle Rick and his friend Bob that gave their all for you. She asked whatever happened to Bob, and Charlie stood tall and said that he just gave himself in trade to save my mother. She is the one with the leg wound. The nurse looked at me and said that he gave himself? Charlie then gave her a brief summation of what has gone on. And she gave him a hug and said that his mother and his girlfriend will be taken care of, you can count on us. Charlie shrunk from the words, girlfriend and the team all came up and said did you not get it that Jenny is nuts over you and would walk on fire for you. Charlie had no words for that statement from them.

They told Charlie that his mother was doing fine and had been transferred to a room and that he could go up. Charlie asked about Jenny and a nurse said she is still in surgery and they will let him know when she is in a room. Charlie thanked her and went to his mother.

He entered her room and she looked as if she was sleeping, but after he entered the room she didn't ask about Bob or Jenny, but she asked about Terri.

Charlie smiled and said that she has so many young strong men watching her now I feel that she will only hope that this goes on for a long time. His mother smiled and then wanted to know of Jenny, he said that she is still in surgery and we should know soon.

Josie looked at him and said that you know son that she is the one for you, and Charlie finally admitted it to his mother that he feels the same about her.

The door opened and in came the commander and he came up to the bed and said to Josie that you know your son and his team has done a remarkable job today. Josie said that she understood some reason of this mission but still wanted to know why no one is going after Bob. He then said that Bob is bait.

Josie then mentioned that fishermen use bait, but we do not. And again, she asks why no one will even try to go after him. Charlie started the conversation with, mom you know that Bob would do whatever he is asked of, because him and Uncle Rick were combatants and that now that he is gone Bob feels that he owes it to him to be with him to save us all.

Uncle Rick help Bob save his family and now Bob feels that he must do the same. Bob told me that in death we are brothers and that's how he feels.

Josie now being on a great number of painkillers, thrashed her arms and said Charlie, Bob will never be with your uncle where he is at, and immediately the commander stepped up and said that your mother needs rest and I will see to it, just go to Jenny. Charlie left and the commander said you need rest and that what you think you know will possibly have people killed, and that could be Charlie. Josie looked at him and with her drugged eyes said but you... and she was out.

CHAPTER THIRTY-THREE

Charlie was sitting at Jenny's bedside holding her hand and smiling at her as she was sleeping. The commander walked into the room and asked Charlie how she was doing and has she been up yet. He said not yet but the doctors say that she should be ok after she wakes up, but will probably be pretty drugged up for a while. Charlie then said like my mom, she was talking crazy, right. The commander said that he has seen many soldiers talk of many weird things when under pain killers. Now Charlie we must talk and you can come back here after she wakes up and you can talk to her, because I know where they will take Bob.

Charlie stood up immediately at what he said and they walked out of the room and sat in the waiting area. No one was around now, mostly because of all the team members that were standing guard by Jenny's room.

These guys were so well equipped today so much more than the other day, mainly because they thought that saving Josie would be a basic snatch and grab, but as they found out it wasn't anything easy about it.

They had a greater number of weapons than anyone felt that they would have, and lucky for us that Jimmy got one that was just about to shoot off a RPG and if that happened, more of us would be here at the hospital or worse. So today they are ready for any type of battle that may be coming our way this time.

The commander said that your uncle had a mission to eliminate a target in a small village in Afghanistan, one that was not even on our maps. It was a roaming type of village that would move with the weather and only in a few different spots. Your uncle went into this operation alone so only limited possibility of being caught.

He lay in a garbage dump for a day, Charlie interrupted him and said that my uncle told Bob this story and told him that it was an upcoming leader, but you wanted him out before he did get bigger in the area.

The commander said yes and that man was Syeed and Aziz's brother Mohammed. So now you see the revenge of those men, and Charlie looked at the commander and now you see my revenge on those men from me. He nodded yes and let Charlie know that we all have an interest in your revenge. And together we will achieve it. Now, let me give you more information of approximately where they may be heading and how we will be able to get him out and at the same time get our target, Syeed.

A nurse came up to Charlie and said that she was sorry for the interruption, but Jenny is asking for you to come in now.

Charlie sprang up and apologized to the commander and took off towards her room. As he was getting closer he started to feel uneasy. He was wondering if she remembered what she said before the drugs took effect on her. For a second he wondered but then he opened the door to her room and when he saw her lying in bed, he only wanted to be with her right now. He entered the room and Jenny had a huge smile and said I thought you would not see me after what I said to you before I went out. Charlie hesitated for a second and then didn't care at all of him being uneasy now because she made him feel so good every day that they are together.

Charlie only could come up with how you feeling and Jenny laughed, even though it hurt. Charlie, get your body over here and gives me a hug, right now soldier. He double stepped to her bed side and bent over and gently gave her a hug. Jenny whispered in his ear, sorry if I scared the big bad soldier with what I said to you before. He looked at her and told her that he felt the same and smiled at her. She started to cry and it was not from any pain, but from what he just said to her, and it was tears of joy. Just as Charlie was giving Jenny a little kiss, in came Jimmy and stopped. Sorry sir but the commander gave me some info on the next mission and I want in sir, if that is all right with you.

Charlie turned to him and said that I would want no other if I had the choice of only one to go Jimmy.

He smiled and almost gave him a hug. Jenny said being still in a little woozy state, why so important.

Jimmy said because we are going to where his uncle shot Mohammed from a trash dump, wild. Afghanistan!

Jenny sat up in bed and gave Charlie a look and it was not a loving one. She asked him when the team is leaving. He said soon, very soon, and she said what about me, aren't you waiting until I get a little better. He said that orders from the commander say you are to get better and be my mother's bodyguard until we get back. She still had a frown on her face, until Jimmy said that they took Bob there and we have no time to wait, sorry Jen, but you do understand. She told them that after you get Bob back I want all of you to promise that Syeed is dead, not just look dead, but real dead. Do you understand soldiers? They both stood at attention and saluted her. Then she said to them what are you two waiting for, you have a mission to attend to, and smiled.

CHAPTER THIRTY-FOUR

As we were driving to who knows where. I asked the driver that if he knows how long until we get to our destination, because I would like to take a nap. One of them turned and said that Syeed wants you alive, but he did not say in what condition, then he hit me hard in the jaw. I almost coughed up my upper teeth and that is not be good since now my jaw hurt and I may not make much sense when I try and tell them where we are going at times. While this was happening, the communications officer was listening and recording every word and sound that he heard from us.

I then told them that I am a very valuable person and that Syeed would be very upset with whoever accidently killed me. They grumbled to each other and just kept driving. I said to one of them that you guys are very good at making sure that no one can follow you. I can't believe how many times that we went off and then back on the highway. Then I said but serious guys are we close because I should go to the bathroom and back here I would make a mess. One said we will be at our site in about 10 minutes, can you hold it.

I then said but we just passed that gas station with a sub shop on highway 10 and I bet it had a bathroom. He just looked at me and said wait.

We did arrive at what was our new home for a short time until we leave again. I was escorted out to a small building that looked as if it was used for some type of machine shop. The business has been gone for some time now, but it was in a secluded location off the highway and with no visible traffic going by it.

Back at camp the person manning the radio heard it all and was trying to get some type of fix in my location, not to come and get me but to track my movement to follow and obtain Syeed if possible. I knew that it would take a miracle to save me and kill Syeed, but that is exactly what I was hoping for right now.

So, I kept on talking in hopes that they were listening and would have my location to follow. Back at camp Charlie walked in and wanted to know what has been going on with our bait. And the radio man said that he is giving almost his exact location with landmarks.

Jenny made it with help to Josie's room and sat with her for a little while, and talked mostly about Charlie. Josie said that she is so happy that Charlie has found such a beautiful and competent partner in her. Jenny answered back with that I want more than a partner and if you will allow me to do whatever I can to have Charlie as my husband someday.

Josie looked shocked at her, but not in a bad way, and told her that you are exactly who my son needs to be with him as his wife. They both smiled and then the phone rang on Jenny's chair; she had a cell strapped to it for emergency calls.

Jenny answered it and on the other end was Samantha. Jenny froze and handed the phone to Josie, because she said that she had no idea of what to say to her now. Josie said hey girl what have you been up to lately. And Samantha answered back that probably a lot less than you guys. Josie had no idea what to say next so she said, how is your mom, and that was a dead giveaway to Samantha that things were not good where they were at. Samantha said besides my dad who else has been shot? Josie handed the phone back to Jenny and told her to be direct to her.

Jenny said that your dad has not been shot, well as much as we know right now. And that Josie was taken hostage and when her son and his team tried to rescue her, that is when she was shot in the leg. And I tried to bring her back to a safer place and that is when I was shot in the shoulder. And that is when Samantha asked so my father is dead then? Jenny said not that we know, and he could be in good shape right now. Samantha then said so he may or may not be dead and that he may or not be around you. Jenny then spoke up and told her that your father traded his life to make sure that Josie's life was saved. And Josie spoke up and said that the whole team is out hunting you for him and that he is the bait to get Syeed.

171

Then Samantha said that my dad has given his life possibly to ensure that the person responsible for Rick leaving us is dead!

Jenny said yes and that he wanted it this way. Samantha said to keep her updated on what is going on and that no matter what the outcome to please be straight with her.

Jenny agreed and then hung up. Josie gasped at what just transpired between all of them.

Jenny then said to Josie that you were right with being direct with what I was telling her, I feel that she has been through so much with her father that nothing phases her on what is happening right now, Josie agreed.

CHAPTER THIRTY-FIVE

Charlie was in deep negotiation with the team over who is to go, and every single member wanted the opportunity to not only save Bob but have their chance of being the one that fired the shot, the one to kill Syeed. Charlie looked at the commander and was hoping that he would help in the decision. He didn't and Charlie kept trying to figure out his new situation. The commander wanted to go over some of the immediate plans to locate Bob and eventually Syeed. Charlie said that a coin flip was out of the question so what he came up with, was not a bad idea at all. He told the team that they will be split up into four units, and each one will have a purpose in the mission, even though they may not have the chance for that shot.

Charlie then pulled out a map and had two areas circled, each one could be where they can be headed to, and that is where the teams come into the plan.

Two units will go to Helmand Province and the other two will go to Kandahar.

Sources of the commander and from past observations of these people, these are the two areas that he may be in.

He is always moving back and forth from these two areas and we do not have perfect information for an all-out strike on one of them. If we are wrong, we will never find Bob or have a chance at Syeed.

Charlie was going over each unit duties when the commander came into the room; he gave Charlie a folder with all the information from the operation that eliminated Mohammed by Rick James many years ago. Charlie held the folder as if it was some type of ancient rare book. He thought to himself that he is holding the last mission that his uncle had completed while still in the military, after this one he left the military for civilian life. In it were the planning and the implementing of the plan to the briefing of the outcome of it.

Jimmy was standing by Charlie and reached out and asked Charlie if he could read the report of his uncles last mission, after all he is Jimmy's sniper hero.

Charlie handed him the report and told him to study where it was and how they got there, also what he feels he needs today to complete a similar mission but with a twist of a rescue along with a target kill. Charlie looked at Jimmy and said that I hope that you have the opportunity for the kill shot. Jimmy nodded and walked away and sat down and opened the folder and with his eyes opening even wider as he read it.

Each of the four units will have a sniper and a spotter for him, which will also be the radio man, and they will have one stealth operator that would stay out front as they moved through the unknown tory. One for each four-man unit and the other duty of them would be to coordinate any type of infiltration of an area that they will be entering, especially if the enemy occupies it. And one to bring up the rear always is checking behind if anyone is following them.

The mission was underway, but the only part of it was when it will start for them. Charlie knew that if they left too early that they might miss in what direction that they are going, and if too late, well they may be just too late. Charlie knew that timing was everything and hoping for some information from me would be helpful, but there has been silence for some time and that worried him. But what he didn't know was that the punch to my mouth made my mouth swell up and it was very hard to talk or even open it.

Jenny called and wanted to know any details that he could give her, she so wanted to be part of this mission. Charlie gave what little information that he felt was not classified material and she let him know that his mother, Samantha, and she are wishing you all the skill to do your job at the highest level. He thanked her and said that he will see her when he sees her.

The plan is ready, and the team is beyond ready.

We are only waiting for a signal or just a word, and we will be off to the plane and make our way to the destination that we hope we will find Bob and the target.

I did everything I could to open my mouth when a man came in with a blindfold, I knew that we are about to leave and I need to get a signal to Charlie. As I opened it, I repeated what he said and that was we are leaving now, to the airport, but we will be going to different locations before we are at the final one. I hoped that someone was listening because that the pain was too great to try and open it again right now.

The radio operator back at the camp where the team was stationed ran as fast as he could to where Charlie was at and while trying to catch his breath, he said to Charlie, there on the move! And so was the team, everyone was up and heading to the plane and they knew that they will be heading direct and that Bob would be going all over to lose any tail that may on them, like us. Charlie only hoped that this plan worked better than the last one.

CHAPTER THIRTY-SIX

Blindfolded and put into a car and driven to some unknown location with my captures. We drove for only about an hour and when we stopped I could smell jet fuel and insecticide, I thought that was a strange combination of odors. After we stopped they removed my blindfold and then I knew the smells, a small jet was on a runway that was mainly used for crop dusters and some private single planes. Now, not a person was around, just the people that I was about to travel with and a pilot.

We all boarded the small 12-person jet, two seats up front and 10 in the passenger area and it was a nice jet. I spoke the best I could for my mouth still hurt, hey guys you know how to impress a person. A jet at a crop plane airport and all the bells and whistles on this jet, even my favorite lottery numbers on it, 28765 SB now that is a coincidence isn't it guys. One man said stop calling us guys! He said that you will be alive but will not be able to ever talk again. I smiled and told them that I get the message.

I hoped that they heard me, because I feel I will out of range soon. The radio man wrote down the numbers and gave it to Charlie and he looked them up to find who owned the jet.

He found out that it belonged to a charity for Middle Eastern people, and that it had no flight plan sent to anyone. Charlie said to the others, I am not happy with this new news we just received from Bob.

The commander was sitting in the back of the room and spoke up and said that with a jet like that even if they do not switch before they head overseas, that they must refuel at least one time before they do. Charlie how many other planes does that charity have registered them besides this one. Charlie said that they a total of four, and one is big enough to cross the ocean to get to Europe and refuel than to Afghanistan.

Now on our plane Charlie said that we should be right this time and the team said, that we will and let's get wheels up and head in his direction that we feel he is heading now. Charlie told the pilot that we are going to New Jersey. Charlie thought how ironic that Bob changes planes miles from his daughter and she will never know. The team all at once said aloud, we are with you Bob, and we took off.

As we flew to our destination Bob was also. He had no idea if anyone heard him; he only hoped that they did and is on their way right behind him.

On the jet, I decided to see if they had scotch, and you guessed it they have no alcohol and then I asked for some water. That they had and after a few sips I knew that my jaw was probably broken and if no surgery I will talk like this until Syeed will swipe my head off or I come home.

I tried to get some sort of idea where we were going to, but they would not let me open the shade on the window. I was getting frustrated but decided to let them feel that I have given up. I sat back and just sipped my water waiting for some type of opportunity to try and send some type of message of where we will be landing.

If it is not out of their range to receive it and I can open my mouth by then.

The team were on their way to New Jersey in hopes of being closer to my where about to receive any message that I sent. And they knew that after that they would have a harder time to locate me unless an Air force Ariel communications plane went up to locate me.

Jenny radioed Charlie in a panic telling him that an attempt on Samantha was just stopped Charlie said it is New Jersey that they are heading to. Now if they had Samantha then they had the daughter of the infidel that they would make her watch them kill him.

Charlie told Jenny to make sure that she is completely protected, even if they must get her to the White House basement. Jenny said have it boss, then she signed off.

Charlie was now a little concerned about the idea that if they wanted Samantha and they did not get her that they would land somewhere else.

And as he had that feeling the plane with Bob landed at a private landing strip in New Jersey and as the plane landed I spoke up as if I was regular passenger on any other commercial plane that was landing, yes! we made it, thank you pilot and thank you my traveling companions, now that we just landed can I see where we are.

One of the men said that you are just a few miles away from your daughter and she will never know that you are here and if things go good, she will be with us soon. I know I was about to panic when another man came into our area and spoke to him and he turned to me and said that he was so sorry, but your daughter will not be with us on this trip; some unforeseen things have kept her from making this flight today.

I sat back and in my mind said thank you guys for that one. I knew that the team that was watching her did their job today.

CHAPTER THIRTY-SEVEN

I joked to one of the men even though they did not like any other things that I said that was funny at least to me, how much longer until we get there, and yes, they did not think it was funny at all. But it did get the attention of one of them and he said to me that we should be to our next destination very soon, I thanked him and turned to another one and asked him the same and he said to me that when you get to where you will be then you will know.

Well the first one was right in that we were starting to land; I could tell by the pitch of the plane and others starting to get ready to put on their seat belts. I knew that we were in New Jersey, but I only hoped that no one would try and rescue me yet. So, as we landed I held my breath and opened my mouth and said one word. Landed!

Unknown to those on that plane another one landed also not far from their location, on another landing strip that was a private strip for a corporation that has military accounts.

Charlie's plane didn't unload but just refueled, they wanted to be ready to take off at any time.

The other one unloaded both passengers and luggage, and transferred all to a much larger jet, one that crosses the ocean without any problem of refueling. Since this is a larger commercial type jet, they had to file a flight plan because they were leaving from a regular airport and not some farmland landing strip and Charlie had everything he needed for this leg of the trip that they are on now.

Once we were on the other plane I noticed something very strange about who was on it. Most of the people looked as if they were no more than tourists, that have been flying around visiting the sites. But they are not tourists in the same way I would be going to say Texas. What I could make out from the way that they were sitting and not saying a word, that these people were planted on this plane, so it would look as if it was normal commercial flight that was kidnapping me and I assume others also, to where I believe will be Afghanistan.

Charlie on the other hand is so prepared to leave that he sat down and called Jenny. He knew that the waiting was about to have him have a heart attack. So, he called the one person who he knew that could calm him down and get him to focus.

Jenny saw the icon on the phone and knew that it had to be Charlie, when she answered it she did make sure it was him before she said to him, you miss me don't you?

And Charlie immediately agreed and said that he wished that she was with him right now because he feels that he is about to lose it.

Jenny laughed at what he just said and reminded him that he is a soldier and that nothing gets him to second guess his own thoughts. Charlie let her know that she is the most important person in his life, along with his family and Bob. She then told him that everything is ok and no other type of problem has come up. She said that Samantha is praying for her father and we are also, she is a strong woman and if I may say, very smitten with Jimmy. Charlie let out a loud yes! and said that Jimmy has a girlfriend.

Everyone on the plane asked who she was and Charlie said that his friend is counting on him to bring her father back to her, no pressure guy, just must save the girl's father and you are in.

The entire plane yelled out and let Jimmy know that each one of us will help you get the girl. Jimmy thanked them and said that we are just friends, and Charlie came back with, that is not what Samantha is thinking.

Jimmy, stopped and said, she is thinking that? Again, everyone laughed, but in a friendship way. Jenny heard the conversation and said that she will relate to Samantha that Jimmy will return to her. They deserve each other and lord knows that girl has been through so much and is about to go through so much more.

Charlie hung up and everyone was slapping Jimmy in fun and just before he hung up, he told Jenny that when this is over and together again, that he wants a more stable relationship with her. She said so do I soldier, and that is when Charlie said to her that he truly did love her and he will return soon. You heard a sigh and they both hung up.

Chapter Thirty-Eight

I always get so nervous when I am about to take off in a plane, and this time was a little more anxious at the idea that this entire plane and probably the crew were made to look good, and now we are off to an unknown location and when we arrive I may be killed on the spot, before anyone could help me. That is not a good feeling of what may happen to me, that I have come up with.

As the plane went higher up, I could feel it shake and some of the passengers started to hold tight on the arm rest and I also did even though I was not worried about dying from a plane crash as much as I was about a beheading, of me. And I only wished that this was a normal flight, so I could have that drink that I so much deserve right now.

I was flying for some time now and started to get anxious of getting up and at least going to the bathroom or how I wished the bar. But these fine fellows that have been watching me for hours would not have of what I asked for and there I sat, without scotch or anything to drink, even water.

And if I did have water they would give me the hardest time on going to the bathroom, that is why they won't let me have any now, only hopefully after we land I can.

We seemed to be descending now and out the window that I can see, no land yet. I feel that we are close to some area that we will be landing at, and if it is to refuel and take off again, if I can relieve myself, I will be so happy. I heard the wheels going down and now I know that is the signed we are landing soon, I only hope that Charlie has not given up or lost me yet.

The plane landed and some passengers got off and some new ones came on, I think that this commercial looking airliner is a terrorist smuggling operation. As I came on the first time the people that came on to it were a mix of people, so that makes me think that they were heading to a destination to train or to complete an assignment.

The others that have come on looked more seasoned in a way, that they did not even look at me, they went right to their seat. The one thing that I hope that comes out of this operation, even if we do not get Syeed, is that we contain, watch, or stop this operation that they have going on now.

Charlie and the team were just continuing to Afghanistan and relying on the Airforce AWAC that is not far away and NSA satellite that is constantly watching this plane every movement that we are in the air.

Charlie asked one last time that if anyone wants to back out of this mission, it will be fine. Not a one wanted to leave, and the only words heard were when it is over it will be over.

As we stopped at different areas in Europe, precisely three different cities in three different countries, some left the plane and some boarded. I was completely sure that this was a terrorist transportation flight, none of the people that came onto this plane were surprised at who was on it and how each reacted to the other, silence with no type of communication at all, not even with their eyes. And now that we are finally about end our journey somewhere in the Middle East, I again wondered if Charlie was not far behind or ahead of us, as he was.

Charlies plane landed a while ago and after everything was unloaded they went back to the plane, to make sure that they had all that was probably may be needed.

After they unloaded all their weapons and radios, plus any type of equipment that they felt they may need. Charlie knew that they had way more than what they could possibly need or carry, but he wanted no man to go without what they felt comfortable having on the mission.

Charlie said to the team that we will go into four different directions and all at some point meet at a point that may be the destination of Syeed's men, and Bob.

He knew that the four-team approach gave them the best way of covering the most ground in the search for Syeed and Bob, plus he knew that once on the ground all the eyes in the sky that they had so far would not be able to follow them.

They all agreed and began getting their weapons ready and making their way to the planned spot that they have in this mission.

Charlie only wished that he had up to date and time information on where I was at right now.

CHAPTER THIRTY-NINE

Finally, they let me go to the bathroom, that must be because we have landed and all the rest of who was on board, including the pilots all left the plane. These guys were not taking any chances that I could escape, or hurt the others in some way. I exited the plane and it was almost dark, I had no idea of where I was at and they seemed to make sure I didn't either. I was escorted to a vehicle and we quickly drove off, I did what I could to get some type of idea of the location I was at now before I said to Charlie and the team if they are still able to hear me what to look for.

The four teams were off to their selected locations and in Charlies team was of course, Jimmy as the shooter and a radio slash spotter for Jimmy, a bad dude that Charlie felt would handle any obstacle that may get in their way on this journey. And an all-around soldier who could if needed take on the position of any one of us, just in case of that person was not able to.

As they left, all the teams immediately turn the radios to my channel and only hoped that I could communicate some way with them.

Charlie knew that so many things could stop the radio from transmitting to them and the one that he did not want to be, was that I was dead.

Well, I wasn't dead but sure wished that I was after the ride in the back seat of a Jeep type of vehicle, after I was tossed from one side to the other and my head hitting the roof on many occasions of this very bumpy ride that they were taking me on now. As they were driving I was doing my best to get some type of glimpse of any landmark of what road or area of where I am traveling right now.

We drove a very long time; I did not know exactly how long or in what direction we were heading. If I guessed the time, I would have to say about two hours and I think we are heading sort of east.

I only wished that at this moment an army of my friends were coming over the hill that was just ahead of us, but that would not happen now. Suddenly coming over the rise just ahead was approximately twenty or more men on horseback heading right towards us. At first I hoped, then that hope quickly disappeared when I saw the one out front and he did not look like Charlie. And what I have seen of Syeed, it was not him either.

So, I waited to see who was coming to greet me, and if they had any other orders than to make sure that I get to my destination alive.

The rolling dust from the riders made it to our vehicle and as it started to clear I could make out a young woman that was the one out front. I was completely confused and thought that a man would be in that position.

Well I was wrong and she was not that feminine type of woman, and when she dismounted the rest did after her. She was in charge, but not in the way a man would want. Now I know why she is in charge and that is she is Syeeds daughter, and the one who will be taking over his group if he is dealt with an unforgiving accident that would make him unable to lead. And yes, at 10 yards or more from me, this person has given me a reason to fear my new surroundings.

She not only was feared by me at this moment, but the men with her. She walked to me and looked right into my eyes and said to me, that with such beautiful blue eyes how can you be such a bad person. I only hoped that the eyes were working, but then she said it is such a shame that you will be dead soon and those eyes will be eaten by my dogs. Now I know that I do not want to be in this place.

Charlie now was on his way to a destination that he felt would be the best place to be to meet up with Syeed and myself.

The other three teams went to where they would meet up with me and that each one of them wanted to have me rescued and Syeed dead.

Charlie and his team walked very slowly to the exact spot that his uncle had shot Muhammed, their brother.

He knew that it was the longest shot to intercept me and Syeed, but knew that he would go back to where he was killed and kill his friend, Bob to make his revenge settled. But Charlie had his own revenge and he would not let that be taken away from him anytime soon.

And as Syeed's daughter came right up to me and the fear from her men and now that fear from me, I finally understand the meaning of true fear today. I did make a very bad mistake and spoke first, she gave me the look that I hope I would not see again. I asked her where is Syeed and when do I die. She looked at me and with a smile on her face, said to me, soon.

The radio man kept trying to locate my signal and after many try's he did it. Now they may soon have something from me, that I may say that will eventually know my exact where about of my location and in what condition that I am in now.

Syeeds daughter touched my face with an ever so gentle pat, then said now we will go and meet my father, and not long after that he will take a sword and slice off your head and his revenge will be complete.

I then spoke again not exactly in the right moment and said to her that Rick's nephew, the man that was the person that killed Mohammed, will soon find you and your father, and after that meeting I feel that Charlie Walters will have his revenge. She then said to me that within a few hours my father will have his revenge and what you say that your Charlie is so far away from us, that you will be dead long before they arrive here.

CHAPTER FORTY

Charlie and his team have been slowly making their way to what they feel is the right location. The three others are now moving into their position and all are waiting for that one command to finish it. Each team knows that they may be in the right or the wrong place and that one of the others will hopefully be in the right one.

One team started to head north to a city in the Helmand Province and another team to one that is directly across from it is the town of Kandahar in the Kandahar Province. One team stayed down south of the first team and Charlie's team headed to the tiny village that has started this whole ordeal now. The village where Rick took his shot and eliminated Muhammed the brother of Syeed and Aziz. Charlie figured that it should take a few hours each to make it to the destination that they were given for this mission.

The first team that went north in the Helmand Province started to encounter light resistance from some area locals just an hour into the mission.

The one that stayed south in Helmand, was also having a little trouble with a more elite type of fighting soldier.

In Kandahar city, only a brief scuffle with a few men, nothing that would cause any alarm with anyone. Charlie on the other hand did not run into any type of fighting force at all heading to their village.

The southern team then reported in that they were seeing an extremely large number of fighters and that they are all heavily armed and seem to be well train, much more than the typical rural fighter. The team leader radioed in that he is now up against about 50 or more fighters and one of his men is dead. He also said that his sniper has been hit but not too bad but bad enough to make him not able to shoot at any distance now. As he was trying to communicate with the rest of the teams, Charlie heard that they were now being overrun and soon his radio went dead. Charlie lowered his head in respect of their lives that they must have just given for this mission.

Now the team in Kandahar city started to get even more fighting and with a much larger number and better trained soldier, the same as the first team south had just encountered and with no other thought of them but that they were killed or captured, with these people, Charlie knew killed. The radio man now radioed that the team leader and the spotter were down and that they were now facing approximately twenty fighters.

He said that the sniper has been getting a very good amount of them as I have, but with our ammo running low and theirs seemingly being brought in by mule, we will not last an hour. At that moment, the radio man said bye guys it was a pleasure as a RPG was fired at their location and their radio went silent.

Now only two teams were left and both were too many miles apart to even think of helping the other. Charlie now figured out what was happening and he did not like it at all. Split up the two farthest teams and then they could attack one without the other being able to help, and after that only one would be left and Charlie knew exactly which one, and with that thought radioed the other team to warn them of what is going to happen, and soon.

As all of this was going on I was being taken from one village to another always changing horses to a vehicle than walking, they were making sure that no one would be able to follow and that if they did it would give them the opportunity to see them and eliminate the force before they could them.

I was becoming very tired and sick from lack of water and rest, I asked if I could have a drink and sit down for a moment, but all I got was, soon you will have all the rest you want.

I knew what she meant and could care less about dying by a sword, but I would like to have some water before I do.

We continued our trip and at one moment the leader came to me with a smile and said we have now eliminated two of your elite teams and are close to the third. I lowered my head and thought how awful it was to die in such a lousy place.

Charlie then heard from the other team and the news was not good. The team leader said that they are now under a complete military attack, and that these are not your average villagers with pitch forks, but well trained and well equipped.

As Charlie was listening to his radio, he could not help but think that all his plans have been off. He knew that he could not guess all the strategies that Syeed would come up with, but he felt that he could stand toe to toe with him on it.

Again, the third team has entered the battle and lost. Charlie could only hope that it was quick for them and that torture was not needed because they already met the end.

Charlie now brought his team together and let them know the outcome of the other three teams. Everyone lowered their heads in remembrance of the soldier's that lost their lives on the field of battle today. Then he said we have not had any trouble, while they all did. I feel that soon we will encounter a force that is much larger than they did, so be prepared men.

CHAPTER FORTY-ONE

As Charlie and his only remaining men moved through the area that would eventually have them end in the same village that Rick took the shot, he started to get that feeling as did his men that this is a set up for them. They all knew the other teams, and each one could out fight ten of these men, but they were outnumbered and out gunned.

Charlie could only guess that they have done their homework as he did and put a plan to counter my plan, for mine was based on revenge and his was also but in his country with his people. I wanted him but made the mistake of going to him instead of him coming to me.

As we entered a small village I knew that this is to be my final journey that I will take and that soon I will be reunited with my friend Rick James and all the trouble that I had will soon be gone. We walked to the center of this tiny village and in the middle stood a tall thin man in his normal dress for the area with a very bushy beard and eyes that were like shark eyes that I could see from where I was, and about a hundred men around him. This man I know is Syeed.

We made it to the man that was the leader of many and his daughter told me to kneel in front of Syeed and praise his greatness. I stood tall and told him that I am about to die and with that I will die with dignity and will not have what is left of my life been done in being a coward. He smiled and said to me that yes you will die but not at this moment, you will die with the nephew of the man that killed my brother and you the killer of my other one. I smiled and said so you understand why I will not bow to you, for you want both our heads to roll as you cut them off, and for that reason I will only say that, you will die before I do.

Syeed smiled and said that his men have now eliminated three teams that were sent to get me and as we speak your friend's nephew Charlie's team is being watched and at my command will be attacked and taken here so you can first watch his team die and then you and Charlie die together.

Now I only hoped that Charlies radio man was tuned into my channel and was hearing what was going on now and that he would take whatever things needed to make sure that his team stayed alive. And he was!

The radio had a lot of static and hard to make out certain words and some complete sentences, but at least some words were coming into us said the man to Charlie. Charlie heard words of Syeed and heads roll, plus that we are being watched. Charlie was trying to figure out how to get out of this area without being killed or captured.

He also knew that if they continued the road that they are on now, something bad will happen to this team just as it did to the others.

Jimmy spoke up and told Charlie to listen before he says a word to us. If I find a good position somewhere close to the center of the village like your uncle did, then with my spotter and radio man will be outside of the village being ready to call in an air strike on it if we fail. And Jimmy said that our front man will stay behind a little to cover all of us if needed.

Charlie then with a smile said, I am the bait just as Bob was right. Jimmy said not bait but a distraction I hope for the rest of us to do what we can to free everyone and hopefully kill Syeed.

Charlie then said that he agrees with the plan and tape a knife to the back of my neck just as Bob had one, and hopefully they will not check in that place and I may have one chance to kill Syeed and Bob and I die with dignity. Jimmy then said neither will die if I have a shot and it hits its target.

And if what we try does not work, then we all go out with pride, the other guy didn't smile at what was said and let them know that with every breath that I have, I will take out as many of these bastards as I can before I go.

Charlie knew that this whole idea had a strong chance of failing and so did the others.

But we all know that what happened to the other teams will be happening to us soon and we must do anything that may work to give some time for the radio man to call in the strike.

And after that not any one of us will care of Syeed or what happens to him after. The only worry that Charlie and I know I do is that, what happens to our families.

CHAPTER FORTY-TWO

Jenny was sitting on a couch with Josie and Terri next to her and across was Samantha and her mother Sienna. Jenny was cracking her knuckles as she usually does when in a very stressful situation. Samantha and her mother asked why were we asked to come here today and Josie also asked that. Jenny said that the commander told me to have all of you here and that he was coming to talk to all of us. Josie then said all of us? And Jenny said that is what he said. Josie now knew that only something very bad has happened to those that went after Bob, and Bob.

Samantha stood up and said to Jenny, what has happened to my dad and I do not want anything that is not truthful. Jenny said to her that she does not know what the commander is going to tell us today. She also said that she has a person on this mission that she loves very much and wants him back unharmed as the others.

Josie put her arm around Jenny and said that she hopes that Charlie comes back to the family but mostly to her. Jenny smiled and thanked her.

Samantha asked what happened with the plan that was to take down all of them. Jenny told them that yes, we thought that what we were planning was going to have a great effect on ending this terror on all of us, but what happened to Bob being taken, and who know what he could be going through now, and what we do know is that he is somewhere in Afghanistan and with the teams that were sent too free him and kill Syeed, that the mission put together will be completed.

Sienna then just sat and did not move in any type of movement that would say that she is upset. She asked Jenny that when a commanding officer summons people like us into one place that it could only be for the reason of letting us know that the ones we care for are no longer with us.

Jenny stood up and screamed that Charlie is not dead and somehow, he will get out of any situation that is about to be told to us now.

Sienna then said, so you agree that bad has come into our lives today. Jenny lowered her head and sat back down waiting for the commander. Samantha cuddled into her mother and Josie said that I know my son and his team members, not one of them would give up the mission, so if no one is saved today, no one is alive either. Every one of them started to cry for all the brave souls that have taken on this mission.

The commander walked into the room, and with his entrance the entire room was silent and he was too.

Jenny stood up to salute him entering the room, but he stopped her and said that you are not a soldier at this moment, but a grieving part of someone's family. She looked at him and said grieving? He said yes because some of your team members will not be coming home alive. Jenny dropped to the floor and cried and Josie sat down next to her on the floor to try and let her know that we are all in this together. That helped a little for Jenny, but not enough for everyone in that room. Samantha stood up and said to him, please give it to us straight and with no bull.

He agreed and started with that, four teams went into Afghanistan to save Bob and to eliminate our threat Syeed.

He began to tell them of how they knew of where Bob was at and the teams plan. He said that even with all the intelligent that we had, we still could not know the moves of our enemy. Out of the four teams, only one is left. These men went onto a mission not knowing the outcome a head of time, giving themselves for the mission. Each one that died on the mission, gave their life for the way of life that we all want.

Charlie made a plan that was in my opinion very good, only the fact that we went to him was my only disagreement with him.

With a soft voice and with a gravel-like sound from her, Josie asked the commander, Charlie, is he dead?

He turned to her and at that moment sat down and began to speak, when Josie broke out in tears and just screamed that her son is dead.

The commander looked at her and said that right now both Charlie and Bob are still very much alive. Then Samantha said and Jimmy? He said yes and Jimmy.

The commander then began to let all in that room that what he is about to tell them is so top secret that it was above even the generals on the ground in Afghanistan. I am going to tell you all something that will make some happy and some mad. I have had a team of some of my old past team members that have volunteered to help in what I believe is a mission to end all mission for them and you. They are not far from the area of where Bob and soon Charlie will be at. Josie asked him why did you not let us know about this special team that you have put together, and he said that he did not put it together, but that someone else with a lot more skin in the game did. Josie tilted her head and asked him who?

The commander began his statement with that of who is involved in this rescue if needed mission. Samantha asked, rescue if needed. He said that this mission was put together in the effort if things went bad and a mission of this type was needed. I have many past members who have come together to make sure that this stand by mission would work.

I have men also from Rick's team and I will say that they will go way beyond what is asked of them for the man that he was to them.

Jenny asked if they will save the team that is left, and Josie asked if they will save her son. Sienna then asked if they will save her daughters father.

The commander said that the person in charge of this mission will do whatever is necessary to have a positive outcome from this mission.

Samantha was leaning forward listening to all the conversation, when she started to lean back and as she did, say I know that the person who oversees this new mission will not give up on any of the team, and Charlie and most of all my dad. Because he has a personal stake in my dad and will give his life over and over to have him safe, am I right commander. He looked at her and with so much compassion in his eyes said that you already know the answer to that, don't you Sam. With the answer of Sam, I knew that my dad was coming home to me soon. Because that is what Rick would call me as he rubbed my head in good luck as he said that we can do it, right Sam. She gave a smile and so did the commander.

CHAPTER FORTY-THREE

Charlie was sitting by a fire that one of the group made, and as he did the team wanted to know what his intentions was and that if he was going to give his life for another. Charlie let them know that Bob was willing to do it and I am also. My uncle gave his all for all of us and I will do what is necessary to have my family safe.

The one man told him that he was going in with him and will not sit back to wait for trouble, and if we go we go together. Charlie thanked him for what he is offering but told him that he is needed much more in helping Jimmy and the radio man, way before he would help me, and when trouble starts and we all know it will, then we all need each other to be able to fight at will. He nodded and said then let's make it interesting for them. Charlie asked how? He said that we have a fire going well knowing that they are probably watching us, and right now for all we know.

So, He said that he will leave now while the fire is high and they would feel that they don't have to watch us as close because of it, and I will make my way to where the village is supposed to be and find a spot and wait.

Wait for you or for finding where they may be keeping Bob, if he is still alive that is, and if not I will watch your movements, he said to Charlie.

Jimmy said to Charlie that the grunt can be the forward observer and the radio man will stay behind, so he should leave also and find a nice cave or something to hide in, so when things get ugly he can call the strike. Charlie agreed with both options that were just given to him. Jimmy said that he will break off not long after we leave here and proceed to where the grunt tells me looks safe. The grunt looked at Jimmy and said for your information, my name is Dan, and the radio man is John. So, when we all die soon, please know our names. Jimmy shrugged his shoulders and said that he is sorry, but that I get my nerves out before I have a shoot, bad humor. Dan said no problem, call me grunt if you make the shot. And John agreed with that and said I will see you when I see you, and slide out of camp with Dan, the grunt.

After the two-left camp, Charlie made sure that he had two bed rolls by the fire looking as if it was two men sleeping. Jimmy made up another, but did not go far away from the camp, because he wanted to wait for what was about to happen here when daylight came.

He knew that if they were to try and kill him right away, then he would be close to take out as many as possible before they overcame them.

It was an hour before dawn and Jimmy slide out of camp, the others reported in that they were within yards of the village and John said he did find a cave that will be good until he is given orders to meet back up and go home or to order an air strike on the village. The same village that will have Charlie, Bob and possible Dan and Jimmy in it. John knew his orders and he would not in any way let the men he had fought with die without honor today.

The sun was up and Charlie was also, he went to the fire and relieved himself to have it look as if he was putting it out so they could all move on. He went to each bedroll and gave it a kick, as in a way to wake them up. After that little charade, he walked to the end of the area that they were at as is he was checking out the area around him.

Charlie did not have to wait very long for the next part of this mission. Twenty or more men came riding on horses down to where the camp was at and started to yell and fire off their weapons in a way of intimidation. Charlie turned in their direction as if he was about to defend himself, but after seeing the numbers of riders, he lowered his weapon and raised his arms over his head.

One man came down to where Charlie was standing and said, you are Charlie nephew of Rick James, the man that killed my uncle Muhammed and Aziz. Charlie had no idea what to say to that and so he just said, yes, that's me.

And the man said that you are to come with me and for your friend's I am sorry, and at that instant they all started to shoot at the bedrolls and after a second felt that they killed them, but they did not check. They all gave a victorious scream and with rifle fire then rode off, with me right behind on a horse and with my hands tied in front of me, I guess so I can ride.

At that moment, Charlie wondered how so many dumb men could have out smarted him so far. Well, he did not have long to find out that answer. They rode for an hour and finally came to a village in a valley with a trash dump by the end of it. Charlie now knew that Syeed wanted to kill both Bob and me at the same spot that my uncle killed his brother. As he entered the village, Charlie only cared for where I was at and not where Syeed was, or anyone of them. He also hoped that Dan and Jimmy were in some proximity of where he was at right now.

We stopped in the center of the village and a young woman all dressed as a warrior came walking to me and told me that she is Syeed's daughter and the niece of Muhammed. Charlie now wanted to know if she was the next in line or just a token warrior. He found out quickly with her ordering all the men around her to do her bidding. She asked Charlie that if your uncle was still alive, that do you think that he would try and save you today.

Now that got Charlie's revenge mode up and he said if, and I do mean if my uncle was here or close by today. You and your men and yes, your father would all be dead in such a short time from now. She looked at him and said, so it is good that he is dead and not able to help you now.

She said that your friend is still alive for now, just as you. And when my father has made his decision on when you are to die and who is first, you both will know.

After that conversation that only made Charlie want his revenge sooner, A tall figure came into the sunlight and stood in the middle of the village, his daughter announced to everyone, welcome Syeed, leader of the war against the west.

CHAPTER FORTY-FOUR

Charlie only wished at that moment that he had his hands free to grab his neck in between them and have his revenge. So instead he walked up to him as far as they would let him, even handcuffed they do not trust me. Charlie laughed to himself because aloud and he would be dead already. He was about ten yards from the enemy that caused so much horror and death in or country let alone what he has done around the world with his followers. With both staring at the other, Charlie broke the stare first. He wanted Syeed to feel that he was superior to him and with that confidence he may just let his guard down long enough for the rest of the team to do some damage, and then Bob and him will be able to escape, I hope.

Syeed smiled at Charlie and said to him, so you are Charlie Walters, the nephew of the man that killed my brother Muhammed, right here, almost in the same spot that I will kill you. He continued with you see I know that you have a strong feeling of revenge of me for what I did to your country and your uncle.

I only wished that I had the opportunity to watch his life leave him as he died. But I was not there and do regret it so much. Now Charlie I will have the pleasure of that with you though.

And now to you, the friend of that Rick James who the two of you went around your country saying you were to save your families, but instead were having that as an excuse to kill my followers. I will have you first watch me take your friends nephews head off and after, yours. Then your revenge will end with mine!

They brought me and Charlie closer together, for what I felt was to have each other say our goodbyes, no but for us to have much closer look at each other's death I assume. Charlie winked at me as we both were sat down on the ground. I was not sure of his intention with that, but I smiled and said that too bad that Jimmy and the rest of the team were not here to help us celebrate our final vengeance on this man.

Charlie said that Jimmy and two others wanted to come here but they had a much more pressing engagement to attend. I smiled and waited for what I hoped would be the firepower that would have us get free.

Syeed's daughter came up to us and said that she has a surprise for us now, and we both could not imagine what it could be. Well, it was not long before the grunt was being walked into the camp, with his hands tied behind his neck. Charlie was starting to get nervous.

After all his planning and to mostly losing to this man, he was about to die at his hand he now feels.

Dan the grunt was set down on his knees in the middle of Charlie and myself. Dan looked at Charlie and said I have a plan to.

Charlie looked at him and said great, do we die together or one at a time. Dan said that I also have a knife tied to the back of my neck as you do and I feel that Bob still does. Charlie smiled and said and Jimmy? Dan said not far away, and ready for my signal.

I on the other hand was not so optimistic about us getting free from this village, especially since they have around a hundred or more fighters and we have what I can count, three with knives. Charlie could only say to have faith that Jimmy is ok and that our radio man has already sent out a message of our situation.

I said by the time anyone can get here we will be dead, and I feel that if we are going to die today that we should make sure that we take as many of these sorry asses with us. Charlie and Dan agreed.

Everyone moved to an area that was where a feast as we could see was happening, and I feel that the meal was for our soon to be deaths.

Dan said that when Jimmy fires his kill shot at Syeed, we will take out our knives and do as much damage as we can while Jimmy takes out as many as he can. When we are, free John will radio for extraction, and if we are over run, then he will request a missile attack on our site.

Charlie looked at me and said that he is so sorry for what I was about to endure here today. And I responded with I could not die with a better bunch of guys. We all laughed at that and bowed to say a prayer for our families.

CHAPTER FORTY-FIVE

As we were sitting on the ground and Dan looked at us, he let us know that it is time, he said as soon as the group of men come up to us we will begin the plan and Jimmy should be shooting and we will be slashing anyone until we can get a gun then free ourselves. And after that we will begin our revenge on these demented humans, and get out of here and get back home to our country, where everyone is free.

I spoke up now and told Dan and Charlie that you will need to cut each other's ropes along with mine to have a real fight. Dan said then Bob when it starts cut my ropes and Charlie will cut yours and one of us will do his. I looked at him and said now that is the start of a plan.

As this group of men came closer, we began to ready ourselves for what we feel will be our last battle. They were about five yards from us when they opened their ranks and in the middle of both Jimmy and John. We all looked at each other and wondered what could be next.

Dan said that we wait for Syeed to be next to one of us and at least end his life for all our revenge.

Jimmy and John were still alive and they had been beaten good which gave us hope that we can still prevail today. Because they are alive and when we bring Armageddon on these people, they will rise to the challenge.

I sat on the spot that Rick made his shot, I only wished that on this day he was here to make one more, and take out Syeed before I die here. I do not want my head to be these men's soccer ball today. But Rick has been gone for some time now, and I soon will be to. My last thoughts went to my daughter Samantha and how I will miss her smiling face and quick humor when we were together.

I looked over at Charlie and the others and said that I have no regrets of what we have done together, they all nodded, and said us too.

A moment later came Syeed and his daughter and many others. He stood above Jimmy and John and smiled at us, then let us know that we will watch him kill our friends before we die and he also said that I will leave for last you Bob, for you were his friend in battle and will witness the revenge that I will finally have, with your death.

Syeed pulled out a long sword and as he raised it up high above Jimmy and John, he spoke I am doing.... then a rifle shot was heard echoing in the valley. I looked over at Charlie and he shrugged his shoulders as with me, who just took a shot.

Syeed had blood spreading through his shirt and with his beady eyes looking up and opening bigger, he dropped back and was dead.

His daughter started to raise her AK47 up towards us when another shot was heard and she was hit and dropped to her knees first and said I am now with you father, and she was now dead also.

Dan pulled his knife and cut Charlies ropes and Charlie his and then mine. We were free and started to fight the captures that are still here. When out from it seemed like everywhere was guns firing and taking out just about every one of his followers. I looked and saw at least twenty fighters all in camouflage and kicking some serious butt, right now.

Charlie yelled towards Jimmy and John, who are they!

One of the soldiers told us that the commander sends his regrets that he could not be here to take part in the dismantling of this terrorist group today.

But he sent us, and we are happy to be here to help you guys.

We all smiled and suddenly some of these men turned towards a few large boulders, and coming through them with the sun behind this man, and with him you could make out that he was carrying a sniper rifle, because of its length.

As this person came closer to us, my mouth opened to speak but no words would come out. And the same for the rest of our team.

And this object that stood before us all, then spoke first, and said nice to see you Bob, and it is a great pleasure you also Jimmy, I am not a ghost but a mere man and not an idol. John and Dan, thank you for being with Charlie and Bob during this mission.

But most of all, I am so happy to see my *Nephew Charlie*, and my friend Bob again. And Charlie today together we have just obtained our families revenge, and did not let them get theirs, and now it finally ends!

This is the third book in the sequel of what happened when terrorists came and tried to take over our country and failed. With the travels of, Bob and Rick to make good of the promise to Bob's daughter and together to find Rick's family and save them, from the remnants of the invaders, to the final chapter in the revenge of a family. Three stories that end in one final ending of a group of American hero's. A Family's Revenge was not Charlies alone, but that of the entire American people. One shot fired, started it and one shot fired ended it. Is this ordeal finally over or does it have one more chapter that has not been told yet!

As the writer of these three books, I enjoyed telling the stories that could be a possibility. We all say that it could never happen to me or in my area. But, small incidents have and may, just be the beginning of my story. A reality for all of us to endure. More books are on my mind, not all like these but different genres, so I do hope that you enjoy the stories as much as I have writing them.

63759835R00124

Made in the USA
Lexington, KY
17 May 2017